"Whoa!" His steadying hands went to her upper arms. "Where's the fire?"

"Oh! Sorry," she mumbled, flustered, feeling as if a low current of electricity trickled through her at the contact. She sought for coherent words. "I–I was looking for the library."

"Is it on fire?" he quipped, raising his brow.

"Fire? No—of course not." Realizing he still held her close, Julie disengaged herself from his hands and stepped back, attempting to gain control. "The maid said you wanted to speak with me there."

He studied her a moment then motioned to an open door a few yards down the hall. "The library. Shall we go inside?"

Offering a feeble nod, Julie followed him. At his signal she took one of two leather wingback chairs in the room. This place was friendlier than the office to which she had first been escorted upon her arrival. A fire crackled in the fireplace, dispelling the chill.

"Is the boy okay?" she asked.

"The doctor has been notified and will be here shortly to check on Jon. He lives close and doesn't mind gracing us with a house call now and then." Jonathan sank into the opposite chair. "I'm indebted to you, Miss Rae. Emily told me everything. Your quick thinking saved Jon's life."

The words were gracious, but the manner in which they were delivered seemed indifferent.

"Your actions have more than aptly shown you're able to take care of the children. In short, Miss Rae, if you still want the job, it's yours."

Julie's eyes widened with a mix of astonishment and relief. Instantly the words she'd heard before the rescue echoed in her mind: *Do not lie to attain your goal.*

PAMELA GRIFFIN juggles her time between writing, home-schooling her two sons, and engaging in all the activities that make a house a home. She fully gave her life to the Lord Jesus Christ in 1988, after a rebellious young adulthood, and owes the fact that she's still alive today to an all-loving and forgiving God and to a mother who steadfastly prayed and had faith that God could bring her wayward daughter "home." Pamela's main goal in writing Christian romance is to help and encourage those who *do* know the Lord and to plant a seed of hope in those who don't.

HEARTSONG PRESENTS

Books by Pamela Griffin
HP372—'Til We Meet Again
HP420—In the Secret Place
HP446—Angels to Watch Over Me

Beacon
of Truth

Pamela Griffin

Heartsong Presents

Thanks to all my dear friends and family who helped me to critique this story. Also special thanks to Paige, her husband, Troy, and their friend Rocky, for answering all my P.I. questions. I dedicate this book with much love and gratitude to my Deliverer, Jesus Christ the True Light Who shattered the world of darkness that I once inhabited, and set me free.

A note from the author:
I love to hear from my readers! You may correspond with me by writing: **Pamela Griffin**
Author Relations
PO Box 719
Uhrichsville, OH 44683

ISBN 1-58660-485-6

BEACON OF TRUTH

Cover illustration by Dick Bobnick.

one

Memories. Some were pleasant, but most were too painful to dwell on for long. She wished they could just be shut away in a box and taken out only when desired. Everyone had told Julie that time would heal the pain. But sometimes she wondered.

She cleared items from the scarred desk, pausing every once in a while to brush her fingertips over a precious memento while reliving the memories. Tears pooled in her eyes as she placed a clear acrylic paperweight into an open cardboard box. Forever imprisoned in the center of the small globe sat a vivid purple butterfly with lemon-yellow spots on its wings. She had given the keepsake to her father on his birthday when she was seven years old. That had been a wonderful day. Later they took his small sloop and fished at a nearby lake.

The intercom on the desk buzzed loudly, startling her. Julie glared at the outdated, intrusive box with its blinking white button. She had told her secretary she wanted to be left alone. Putting out her hand, she pressed the button. "Yes, Tina. What is it?"

"Sorry to bother you, Miss Daniels, but there's a woman here—and she insists on seeing you."

Julie drummed her fingers on the cluttered desktop. Couldn't anyone leave her to her grieving? "Tina, you know that we—I mean, I—am not taking any more cases."

A short pause ensued before Tina's voice came back over the speaker, lower this time. "Miss Daniels, I know you're going through a hard time right now, but the woman says you're the only one who can help. She's really upset about something. And, well, frankly I don't think she'll leave until she talks to you."

Julie let out a loud breath. "Okay, fine. I'll see her. But

5

give me a couple of minutes first."

"Yes, Miss Daniels."

Julie looked at the mess on the desk. Her father had never been one for neatness. She gathered the remaining sheaves of papers, receipts, and countless personal effects and tossed them into a cardboard box, which was then shoved toward one of two filing cabinets. The aluminum balls from myriad sticks of spearmint chewing gum were swept into the trash. She would go through the box later, in the privacy of her apartment.

In the adjoining bathroom, she rinsed her face with cool water, hoping to erase any traces of tears. Looking up into the water-spotted mirror, she surveyed her appearance. Her brown eyes were still red-rimmed, but she couldn't do much about that. Unsightly red blotches from weeping still covered her face. She didn't wear makeup, except for lipstick and nail polish, but she wished for some powder now.

Julie straightened the collar of her pink blouse and smoothed her white rayon slacks. She wasn't dressed for business, but she hadn't expected any. Heading back to her father's desk, she slipped her bare feet into white sandals and reached for the intercom. "You may send her in now, Tina," she said firmly, hoping her voice sounded more professional than she appeared.

The door to the outer office opened, and a woman hurried in. Julie wondered if she'd been standing at the door the entire time. Her hair was immaculate, without a single platinum strand out of place. Styled in a sleek chignon, it emphasized an oval-shaped face. Her clothes undoubtedly bore expensive designer labels.

Julie stood and shook the woman's slim, cool hand. "Good afternoon. I'm Julie Daniels. Won't you be seated?"

The woman did so, then leaned forward, clutching the arms of her chair. "My name is Claire Vanderhoff, and I need your help." A frown marred her smooth forehead.

"I'm sorry. I believe my secretary already told you that we— I—am not accepting any more cases. The investigative agency of Daniels and Daniels is officially closed." Julie's voice

cracked on the last word, and she paused to regain her compo-
sure. She would not break down in front of anyone, least of all
this woman who now regarded her with a studied look from
her yellow-green eyes, reminding Julie of a watchful cat.

Locating a stubby pencil, Julie wrote a few names on a
stick-it pad, tore the top sheet off and folded it. "But I can
give you the names of other reputable detective agencies in
the area that might be of service to you." She offered the
paper to the woman. Miss Vanderhoff ignored it, and Julie
allowed her hand to drop to the desk.

"It's your services I require, Miss Daniels. You've been
recommended to me by friends. And not only that, but I saw
a news article months ago, telling how you and your father
captured one of America's most wanted criminals. . . ."

Julie thought back as the woman talked. Though most of
their cases had been mundane or tedious—trailing the wife
of a jealous husband; looking for missing people, mostly children; investigating insurance claims and the like—one of their
cases had held an unusual twist, receiving high notoriety.

Over two years ago Daniels and Daniels had searched for a
man who hadn't paid alimony or child support for years and
had also disappeared. Julie's legwork had led her to the home
of Stanley Smith, also known as Stephen Cordova, wanted by
the FBI for suspected murder, drug trafficking and armed rob-
bery. Julie's brush with danger had helped her find the Lord,
but the frightening event had also contributed to her father's
massive heart attack.

After Smith's arrest, Daniels and Daniels received nation-
wide publicity in their small town of Locklin. News of their
reputation spread, until they had so many would-be clients
that they had to pick and choose. If their services hadn't been
in such demand and their workload hadn't increased dramatically, perhaps Julie's father, who had found it hard to refuse
anyone, would still be alive today.

"I'm sorry, Miss Vanderhoff," Julie interrupted the woman,
who was still pleading with her to take the case. "But my

father and I were a team. I did the legwork. He was the brains behind our outfit. I really can't help you."

The woman responded by pulling a picture from her wallet and handing it to Julie. Reluctantly she accepted the mini photo.

Two beautiful children with bright eyes and laughing smiles looked back at her. The girl, about six, was blond and fair with matching dimples and light green eyes; the boy, around three, had dark unruly curls and twinkling blue eyes promising mischief. Julie looked up, curious.

Miss Vanderhoff took a deep breath. "The girl is my niece, Emily Taylor, and the boy is my nephew, Jonathan. They're my sister's children. My sister was killed over a year ago, and I feel their lives may be in danger now, as well."

Julie's brow arched at this bit of information, but she waited for the woman to continue.

"Because they found alcohol in my sister's blood during the autopsy, the ruling was accidental drowning—but I know better. The boat was recovered and found with a hole in the bottom—small enough not to be noticed until it was far from shore. But Angela wouldn't have taken a boat on the water without checking it first. And certainly never during a thunderstorm!" Her eyes flashed. "My sister was a great swimmer. She could have managed with no problem—unless, of course, she was unable to. Mark my words—Jonathan killed her as sure as I'm sitting here! Those people were fools to drop the charges against him."

"Jonathan?" Julie stared at the irate woman then at the picture.

"My sister's husband. The boy was named for him."

Julie nodded. "There are other agencies which can be of service. As I said, I cannot help you."

"Oh, but you just have to!" The woman threw her hands out to the side, causing her diamond-crusted emerald ring to flash in the overhead light. "You're the only woman detective I know in this area with a better than reputable standing."

"What does my being a woman have to do with anything?"

"Jonathan has been practically a recluse since my sister's death. He won't let the children leave the mansion and has forbidden visits from relatives or friends. Recently the children's governess quit or was fired—I don't know which. Employees rarely last long at that place." Miss Vanderhoff leaned forward. "I happen to know he's looking for a new governess now. That's where you come in. You could take the job of nanny and be in the house, both to keep an eye on the children and to discover the truth about my sister's murder."

"But I don't know anything about being a nanny! I never had any brothers or sisters—in fact, I know very little about taking care of children at all."

"That's unimportant." The woman waved Julie's concerns away with her hand. "I have references for you that would assure you of getting the job. They're good, well-behaved children—I mean, it's not as if they're in diapers or anything. Have you ever babysat?"

"When I was in high school, but—"

"I'm sure you'll do fine. Here's the address." She placed a slip of paper on the desk as though Julie had agreed to take the case. "They live on the coast of Maine, a few hours' drive from Portland. I'll arrange for plane reservations and take care of any monetary needs you have in association with this job, as well as a handsome salary. I have more than enough money to cover everything."

Julie gave an exasperated sigh, her patience stretched thin. "Even if I were to agree to go undercover for you, I don't like the idea of giving phony references. I don't like the idea of lying." The woman raised her brows, and Julie knew the admission had shocked her. Good. Maybe now she would leave. Julie leaned back in her chair. "I'm sorry, Miss Vanderhoff, but as I've already told you, I cannot accept this case."

Julie was beginning to feel like a parrot. And like a parrot her words were scarcely heeded as being of any real importance.

The woman shoved the picture back at Julie. "Surely you'd make an exception to save the lives of these precious children."

Julie looked at the cherubic faces in the photo and felt her heart soften. Most likely the woman was exaggerating and the children were in no danger. But what if they were? Could Julie live with herself if something terrible happened to them, when she might have been able to prevent it? But taking the job of a nanny? What exactly did nannies do? Still, it couldn't be so hard, could it?

After struggling inwardly with conflicting emotions, Julie handed the picture back to Miss Vanderhoff. "All right. I'll help you." Her tone was resigned.

The woman visibly relaxed into the upholstered chair, a victorious smile sweeping across her face.

"But," Julie continued, "I want to make it perfectly clear I deal only with facts and truth. I don't base my final judgment on assumptions. Whether Jonathan Taylor murdered your sister or not is still to be proven in my eyes. If I come to the conclusion that he's innocent, then you'll have to abide by that decision."

The woman grudgingly nodded.

"All right, then," Julie said, opening a notebook and grabbing a pen. "We have much to discuss. Would you like some coffee before we begin?"

After Claire Vanderhoff left forty minutes later, Julie snapped on her intercom. "Tina? Please come in and bring your steno pad."

Once her secretary was seated, Julie began. "Get Dale on the phone," she said, speaking of her former chief operative, the "tough guy" every investigative agency needed. "His new job doesn't start for another month, and he might be willing to help us out on this one. I want any and all information on Claire Vanderhoff, the woman who just left my office, and a full bio on Jonathan and Angela Taylor from Breakers Cove, Maine. Incidentally, Angela is deceased. I need anything and everything—birth records, school records, misdemeanor charges—"

"The name of their best friend's cat?" Tina asked with a grin. It was an old joke at the office, a compliment to Julie that she left no stone unturned.

Julie cracked a smile. "Yeah. Okay. You get the picture. Also find out if I'll need to obtain a permit to practice in Maine, and take care of any paperwork not requiring my signature. Get me reservations on the first flight going out tomorrow. I need to get home and pack and—what?" Julie asked, her gaze again landing on Tina's face, which was now beaming.

"It's just good to have you back, Miss Daniels."

Julie stiffened. "This is the final case, Tina, and I felt bamboozled into accepting it. So don't get your hopes up."

Tina nodded. "I'll get right on this for you."

After her secretary left, Julie looked at the opposite wall where a framed print hung, one she had ordered through a catalog. A lighthouse emitted a golden beam on a murky background of dark sea and sky, and the words underneath proclaimed: "The light of God shall burn brightly, cutting through the darkness and revealing the hidden secrets and mysteries therein."

When Julie first spotted the picture in the catalog, she'd known it was perfect for the detective agency. She saw herself as an ambassador for Christ, helping to bring to light the dark deeds of men and see to it that they received the justice they deserved. As she stared at the painting now, she prayed God would once more equip her with His beacon of truth in this final assignment—one that promised to be the most challenging of her career.

❧

Clutching her suitcase, Julie stood watching as the taxi drove down the narrow winding road toward the tall iron gates at the estate entrance and disappeared beyond the trees. *I should have had him wait,* she thought, mentally kicking herself. *Suppose I don't get the job?*

She turned her attention to the jagged cliffs and towering evergreens that covered the remote area. A massive two-story wood and stone house with gables and numerous multi-paned windows stood above her, outlined against the ash-gray sky. Flanked on three sides by white pines and golden maples, the monolith faced the Atlantic Ocean. To Julie's right, the sea churned against a large outcropping of rock, sending up showers of white spray. As breathtaking as the setting was—like something from a picture postcard—it emitted a formidable atmosphere. Julie felt as if the house itself had already rejected her.

This is silly! I'm letting my imagination get the better of me. Pulling her linen suit jacket closer around her middle with one hand, she hurried up the steps. A ring of the doorbell soon revealed a tall, middle-aged housekeeper, who narrowed her eyes in an icy stare. She fit the place well.

"I spoke with you on the intercom outside the gate," Julie said. "I'm here about the advertisement for a nanny." When the woman didn't respond, Julie held out the newspaper opened to the classified section with Jonathan Taylor's ad circled in red. She had been relieved and somewhat surprised to run across it. All during the plane ride she had debated how to broach the subject of a job, unaware he'd advertised in a local paper. "My name is Julia Rae," she added, giving her first and middle names.

The woman stared down her nose at Julie through a pair of silver-rimmed spectacles matching her hair. Her gaze dropped to the battered suitcase sitting beside Julie, and she frowned. "Do you have an appointment?"

"No—I just got into town today. If Mr. Taylor isn't busy, I'd like to see him. Barring that, I'll have to use your phone so I can call a taxi. The one that brought me has left."

"Wait here. I'll see if he's available." She shut the door in Julie's astonished face.

Julie stood shivering on the porch while almost five minutes elapsed, according to her wristwatch. She could have at least let her stand by the door on the inside! Though the cab driver had mentioned how mild the weather was this time of year by

Maine's standards, Julie, who had lived most of her life in Florida, felt the cold intensely.

The door opened, and the woman motioned Julie inside. She followed the housekeeper into the foyer and down a hallway to a medium-sized room where she was told to wait. After giving Julie one more look of disapproval, the woman disappeared into the hall and shut the door.

Julie eyed the dark paneled walls, the unlit fireplace, the scarred black walnut desk with a computer console on top, the muddy brown furnishings, the cluttered bookcases—obviously an office. Just as the outside of the house was, this room, too, felt remote, cold.

Soon the door opened, and the master of the house strode inside. He could be no one else. The very set of his broad shoulders and lift of his square chin exuded authority and gave an impression of power—barely contained. An inky-gray turtleneck matched the color of his eyes and served to outline every muscle in his arms and chest. His hair gleamed black as midnight and was lightly shot with premature silver strands at the temples—which did nothing to detract from his looks, but rather intensified them. His face held strong yet classic features blending perfectly with his powerful physique.

"Good afternoon," he said, his voice as deep and silky as Julie expected it to sound. "You wish to speak with me?"

Feeling much like the lowly peon confronting the lord of the castle, Julie stood speechless, managing a nod. He motioned to one of two chairs facing the desk.

"Please, have a seat."

She did so, watching as he sank into the leather chair behind the desk with a languid grace, much like a panther resting after a long night's hunt. His gaze rested on Julie's face, and she swallowed nervously at the strangely forbidding look in his eyes. Though he was polite, it was obvious he didn't particularly want her there.

This house was perfect for him. Both the man and his residence had strong lines and beauty, but both seemed remote and untouchable as if a sign were posted saying, "Keep Out!"

His gaze scanned her slight form in the sand-colored linen suit and navy blouse, then roamed her fresh face and short, curly hair. It was obvious by the look he gave her that he wasn't impressed. "My housekeeper tells me you're here about the ad in the paper. You're a bit young, aren't you?"

"I turned twenty-eight last November. It's because of my height that I'm often mistaken for a teenager," Julie explained, accustomed to this type of aggravating comment.

He looked at her thoughtfully. "Are you certain you'll be able to handle two often-rambunctious children? My daughter isn't much smaller than you are," he said, doubt evident in his tone.

Julie lifted her chin with a confident air. "I may be only five-two, but I'm stronger than I look. I participate in many athletic activities which help give me a higher endurance level." Julie made it a point to keep her body well toned with aerobics, jogging, and self-defense classes. Surely, two small children wouldn't be such a problem.

He nodded, seeming satisfied with her response. "Very well. You'll need to be in shape to keep up with those two. They're a handful at the best of times." He paused. "I assume you have references."

Julie tensed. Though deception was a normal part of a detective's work, she felt uncomfortable stating an out-and-out lie. She had used that ploy in her job before she'd become a Christian but shied away from such tactics now whenever possible. Which meant she had denied Miss Vanderhoff's phony references—choosing instead to trust God to go before her and provide a way.

"No. No references."

Mr. Taylor raised his eyebrows in surprise. "I'm sorry, Miss Rae, but under the circumstances—"

"Please, give me this chance," Julie interrupted. "I love children and will do my best where yours are concerned. I don't smoke or drink—"

"I am sorry," he said, overriding her plea and rising to his feet. "But I can't give you the position without proper references. Now, if you'll excuse me, I have pressing business I need to get back to. My housekeeper will see you to the door."

She rose mechanically and followed the sour-faced woman who suddenly appeared at the entry. Within a minute Julie found herself outside on the doorstep. It came to her that she had no way to reach the airport and could hardly walk the distance on the muddy road to the nearest town, toting her luggage. She should have asked to borrow the telephone for a taxi, but in the face of Mr. Taylor's immediate rejection, she hadn't thought clearly.

She grimaced. What was wrong with her? She wasn't a quitter! She needed time to think things out, maybe take a walk by the ocean and plan her next move. How could she get him to reconsider? With the little she'd seen of Jonathan Taylor, such an occurrence would take a miracle.

Pulling the edges of her jacket tighter about her, Julie hurried down the steps, leaving her suitcase behind for the moment. Keeping her arms crossed around her waist, partly for warmth, partly for comfort, she picked her way down the hill.

Lord, I thought this was where You wanted me. I felt I was supposed to help those children. Did I miss You? Or is there some other angle You want me to use besides going undercover as a plant in this house? What should I do now?

Instantly a thought came to her as swiftly as the wind that whipped strands of hair into her eyes: *Trust me; it is My will that you are here. But do not lie to attain your goal.*

Seconds later, a scream ripped through the air.

Turning her head sharply to look over her shoulder, Julie saw a little girl kneeling on a huge boulder at the water's edge and clutching the wet rock with both hands. A dark head bobbed on the water then disappeared.

Julie raced toward them, dropping her purse and stripping off her jacket as she ran. She kicked off her loafers and jumped from the rock where the girl perched. The frigid water robbed Julie of breath, and for a moment her chilled limbs refused to obey what her brain told them to do.

She dove under the frothing water, searching for the victim, then came up for a gasping gulp of air. After another try her hands came into contact with a small body, and she saw that the jacket was caught on the rocks, pinioning the child. She grabbed hold of the slight figure and pulled, hauling the small body close. Breaking the surface of the water, Julie managed to swim to a large, low rock a short distance away. She pushed the unconscious child up onto the semi-flat boulder and, with some difficulty, hoisted herself up next to him.

Her limbs protested, and Julie wanted nothing more than to collapse on the hard, slick surface and close her eyes. But there wasn't time for that. She put her fingers to his neck and found a weak pulse. Seeing the boy wasn't breathing, she turned his head sideways and straddled his legs, moving her hands to his upper abdomen. With the heel of her hand she pushed in quick upward thrusts, forcing the seawater from his lungs.

The girl stood silent above them, transfixed, fear evident in every line of her trembling body. Julie took a precious few seconds to glance up and snap out, "Get help—quick!" Instantly the child took off, her blond braids streaming behind her.

The boy started to make choking sounds and then began coughing, much to Julie's relief. She wouldn't have to administer CPR since he was now breathing on his own. His eyelids flickered, and she found herself looking into a pair of very scared, brilliant blue eyes—full of unshed tears. The same eyes that had smiled at her from Claire Vanderhoff's picture.

Trembling, he lifted his weary arms to her. Julie drew the boy close, holding him on her lap. He cried, his teeth chattering. Slowly she began to rock him and hum a soothing lullaby, while the icy wind drove relentless fingers through their wet clothing. She tried to cover him with her hands and arms and warm him as best she could, though such a feat was impossible, as chilled as she was. Too shaky to stand, Julie decided it would be better to wait for help to arrive than try to make it all the way back to the house with the boy. Surely it wouldn't be much longer until someone came.

Rapid footsteps pounded the ground and scattered rocks. Julie turned her head to meet Jonathan Taylor's shocked and angry gaze as he closed the distance between them.

She closed her eyes and prayed.

two

"What is the meaning of this?" Mr. Taylor addressed them after reaching the boulder, his expression as turbulent as the ocean had become.

Julie was about to respond when the boy in her arms gave a shudder she didn't think was entirely due to the cold. "I s–slipped and f–fell in," he said through chattering teeth.

"You've been warned to stay away from the water when no adults are with you, Jon. You disobeyed a direct order." Mr. Taylor's gaze roamed over the shivering child, moved to encompass Julie's sodden form, then snapped back to Jon. "We'll talk more about this later. This is obviously not the time or place."

He scooped the boy out of Julie's arms. His gaze dropped to her. "Come. You'll catch pneumonia out here in your condition."

Julie forced her chilled limbs to obey and followed Mr. Taylor, who carefully stepped onto the next rock, then to solid ground, and hurried upward to the house, carrying the boy.

Inside, the housekeeper gave a startled gasp upon seeing the motley and drenched pair. Mr. Taylor issued a few curt orders, and she hurried to draw Jon a bath. Emily stood silent on the landing, clutching the bottom of the rail, her anxious gaze never leaving her brother's pale face. A second maid led Julie upstairs to a guest room with an adjoining bathroom.

The young woman put a blanket around Julie's shoulders and moved to run Julie a bath. While she listened to the sound of water rushing over porcelain, Julie clutched the blanket around her shivering form and took note of her surroundings.

The room was decorated in soothing mints, soft blues, and neutral creams, with white pine furniture scattered all around. Against one wall a full-sized bed stood, with a dresser and attached oval mirror opposite. A white-painted desk and chair

18

faced one of two windows in the room. Julie bunched her soggy, hose-covered toes in the luxurious carpet woven in a texture of matching colors. "Nice," she muttered with approval.

The squeak of pipes interrupted her inspection as the maid turned off the faucets and exited the steamy bathroom. "I'll find you a change of clothes while you soak. Oh—and just hand me your wet things through the door, and I'll run them through the washer and dryer."

"My suitcase is outside," Julie flung over her shoulder as she quickly headed toward the heated room. "My shoes and jacket and purse are too—near where it happened. I'd appreciate it if you could get them for me." It probably hadn't been too smart to leave her belongings there, but her mind had been focused on the boy at the time.

Her wet clothes stuck to her like a second skin, but she managed to peel them off and hand them through the door to the maid. After turning the lock, Julie padded over the lush throw rug to the tub. A haze of steam rose off the water, and she stuck her fingers in to test the temperature. Perfect!

Immersing herself deep into the hot, calming water, Julie released a grateful sigh. The silky warmth exuded the sweet fragrance of hibiscus, a tropical haven after her icy plunge into the Atlantic. Briskly she washed the sea salt from her hair with a nearby bottle of shampoo and then sank low until her ears were submerged and all sound was muted.

She rinsed her hair with clear water from the faucet and reluctantly reached for the towel. It would have been nice to turn on the hot faucet again and revel in the bath until her palms and the bottom of her feet shriveled. But she was an unwanted guest and supposed she shouldn't stretch the bonds of hospitality to their limits.

Julie dried herself off with the fluffy towel provided. After wrapping and tucking it about her, she padded to the adjoining bedroom. A rose-colored velvet robe lay on the bedspread. Thankful to the maid who must have brought it, Julie exchanged the damp towel for the plush robe. On the pocket the looped letters "A T" were embroidered in gold thread.

A knock on the door preceded the maid. "Mr. Taylor wishes to see you in the library when you're finished." She handed Julie's things to her and smiled when she saw her wearing the robe. "I'm sure he won't mind if you keep that, but don't let Mrs. Leighton know. She thinks his wife hung the moon and stars, though she's dead now, poor woman. I spotted the robe in a sack waiting to be given to Goodwill. But I'll bet my last dollar the old crow didn't put it there." She gave another friendly smile. "You'd best hurry. Mr. Taylor doesn't like to be kept waiting."

After the maid left, Julie glanced at the robe. Suddenly it didn't feel as comfortable as it had. Julie put on a pair of cocoa-colored slacks and an ivory blouse from her suitcase and pulled a comb through her tangle of damp curls. She glanced at the digital clock on the bedside table and wrinkled her brow. She didn't want to annoy the head of the household with tardiness and sped from the room, down the stairs, and around the corner—to run into Mr. Taylor coming from the opposite direction.

"Whoa!" His steadying hands went to her upper arms. "Where's the fire?"

"Oh! Sorry," she mumbled, flustered, feeling as if a low current of electricity trickled through her at the contact. She sought for coherent words. "I—I was looking for the library."

"Is it on fire?" he quipped, raising his brow.

"Fire? No—of course not." Realizing he still held her close, Julie disengaged herself from his hands and stepped back, attempting to gain control. "The maid said you wanted to speak with me there."

He studied her a moment then motioned to an open door a few yards down the hall. "The library. Shall we go inside?"

Offering a feeble nod, Julie followed him. At his signal she took one of two leather wingback chairs in the room. This place was friendlier than the office to which she had first been escorted upon her arrival. A fire crackled in the fireplace, dispelling the chill. Deep maroons, dark umbers, burnished bronzes, and gleaming golds from the furnishings lent their own warmth without causing the room to look dreary. One long paneled wall was covered from floor to ceiling with books, and a wooden door led to what was clearly a garden at the back of the house. Through the open curtains Julie saw neat rows of shrubbery.

"Is the boy okay?" she asked.

"The doctor has been notified and will be here shortly to check on Jon. He lives close and doesn't mind gracing us with a house call now and then." Jonathan sank into the opposite chair. "I'm indebted to you, Miss Rae. Emily told me everything. Your quick thinking saved Jon's life."

The words were gracious, but the manner in which they were delivered seemed indifferent. Of course, the New England monotone with its abrupt and incomplete sounding words was still strange to Julie. Perhaps that was why she felt that way. Or maybe it was because of the serious stare he gave her.

"I'm thankful I remembered what to do," she said. "I was a lifeguard during the summer of my junior year in high school."

He nodded thoughtfully. "Your actions have more than aptly shown you're able to take care of the children. In short, Miss Rae, if you still want the job, it's yours."

Julie's eyes widened with a mix of astonishment and relief. Instantly the words she'd heard before the rescue echoed in her mind: *Do not lie to attain your goal.*

She took a deep breath and held it before letting it out slowly. "Mr. Taylor, I do want the job. But there's something you should know. I've never worked with children."

He didn't look as surprised as she thought he would. "I appreciate your honesty," he said after a moment. "And I'm willing to try you out for a probationary period, if that's agreeable to you. If after one month I'm not satisfied with your work, I'll let you go. Agreed?"

Julie nodded in relief. "Agreed."

"To be honest, I had been employing nannies through a

local agency, but after receiving a line of incompetent fools, I decided to dispense with the agency's questionable assistance and find my own." He smiled. "So far I'm pleased with what I've seen. You have shown that you have courage and are willing to put yourself on the line for the children."

She released a breath she wasn't aware she'd been holding and returned his smile.

"Now—along the line of job duties," he continued. "You'll be expected to stay with the children throughout the day, except during their nap times. Once they go to bed for the night—bedtime being two hours after dinner—your time is your own. As for schooling I don't expect you to teach them. They have a tutor who will return in August to resume lessons. Your job, simply stated, will be to supervise them, to be a companion, and to see to it that they make it promptly to meals. Any questions thus far?"

"I'm to have no day off?" How was she to proceed with the investigation, with only a few hours here and there to do it?

Mr. Taylor frowned. "I realize that may seem harsh. But at this time if you take a full day off, there's no one to watch Emily or Jon. Knowing that, if you'd rather not take the job—"

"Oh, no," Julie quickly inserted. "I'm okay with it. I just wondered." She also wondered who had been watching the children before she came along but didn't ask.

"If you should need Mrs. Leighton to relieve you for a short time, and she has no other duties, you have my permission to make the necessary arrangements. She dotes on those two and wouldn't mind, I'm sure. Just don't make a habit of it." He leaned back. "Now let's discuss salary."

He named an amount that seemed quite generous. Uncomfortable with accepting income from him while taking money from her client, Julie was glad when the interview was over.

Mr. Taylor rose from his chair. "I'll take you to meet the children now."

Butterflies played spiral tag in her stomach as she followed him upstairs. They walked down a hallway, past the room she had used, and stopped at a partially open door to a playroom. Two pairs of curious eyes looked up at the adults' entrance. Immediately the children quit playing with their toys and sat waiting. They were older than they had been in Miss Vanderhoff's picture. From the bios Julie knew Emily was eight and Jon had just turned six.

"Emily, Jon, this is Miss Rae. She'll be your new nanny, now that Miss Clifford has left us."

Emily stood silent, not a flicker of emotion on her face. Jon responded with a whoop of joy. Jumping up, he ran to Julie and threw his arms around her hips, making it clear he was in favor of the arrangement.

"Jon!" Jonathan's deep voice cut the air. "That is no way to act. Apologize to Miss Rae this instant. She'll think you're nothing more than a wild animal."

Julie wanted to intercede when she saw hurt flicker in the boy's eyes and heard his pitiful "I'm sorry." But this wasn't the proper time to say anything. She had, after all, just been hired on probation. Julie kept her peace but gave the boy a slight wink and smile. His answering, uncertain grin touched her heart.

"I'll leave you to get acquainted," Jonathan said. "Dinner is at six o'clock sharp." Without another word he left.

Nervous yet relieved to be alone with her charges, Julie sank onto the shag beige carpet to get more to their level. Jon dropped down beside her, all smiles. His dark blue bathrobe gaped at the front, revealing a Sesame Street undershirt. The lopsided belt of the robe trailed in a series of loops to the floor. She tousled his damp hair.

"I'm glad to see you've bounced back, Jon."

His blue eyes gleamed. "I was a pirate searching for buried treasure."

"If it wasn't for her, you'd be a dead pirate," Emily said, her words clipped. Jon lowered his head.

Julie turned to take her first good look at the girl. Her

green eyes were full of dislike, tempered with something akin to grudging gratitude. White-blond hair was captured in two long braids, with thick bangs covering her forehead. Her thin arms were crossed, and she stood with her head tilted to one side. She wouldn't be an easy one to win over.

Julie smiled at Emily but received no smile in return. "I'll need your help—both of you." She continued to smile, though it now felt frozen into position. "I really don't know much about taking care of children. Maybe you could help me along by giving me an idea of what your other nannies did?"

Emily's eyes narrowed in a calculating look. "You mean you don't know anything at all?"

"That about sums it up."

Emily studied her a moment then uncrossed her arms and dropped to her knees, now at eye level with Julie. "Oh, it's real easy. First, you must remember never to send us to bed before ten o'clock. And don't make us eat all our greens before we get dessert. Oh—and you mustn't yell at us or force us to do anything we don't want to do."

Julie gave her a steady stare. "I saw that movie too, Emily, though the dialogue was a bit different. *The Sound of Music,* right?"

Emily rolled her eyes and stood to her feet. "Oh, well. It was worth a try. I'm going to my room."

"Should I start checking my chairs for pine cones and my pockets for frogs?" Julie murmured as she watched the girl leave. How would she handle that one? Feeling a tug at her slacks, she turned her head and looked down into Jon's dancing eyes.

"Aww, don't mind her, Miss Rae. I like you."

Julie smiled. "I like you too, Jon. And you can call me Julie if you want to."

The boy jumped up and down with delight. "Julie! Julie! Julie!" he shouted.

She chuckled. Well, at least there would be no trouble with this one.

꩜

A few minutes before six, Julie found her way to the dining room. The table was laid out, replete with steaming dishes of delicious smelling food. Jonathan sat at the head, waiting. He raised his eyebrows in question. No one else was sitting at the table.

The children! It was her duty to see that the children made it to dinner.

Heat rushed to her face, and Julie did a complete round-about, speeding up the stairs. She shouldn't have lain down for five minutes. How could she have known five minutes would turn into more than an hour? She had probably missed the doctor's visit to Jon.

She threw the door of the playroom open. It was empty, toy soldiers scattered over the carpet. Frustrated, Julie wondered where to look next. She hadn't yet been given a tour of the mansion and didn't know the layout of the rooms.

Children's soft laughter floated down the hall. Julie followed the muffled giggles to a closed door, noting it was only two doors down from her room. After knocking softly to announce her presence, she stepped inside.

Emily lay on her stomach atop a pink, ruffled canopy bed, a sketchbook in hand. At Julie's entrance she slammed the cover shut and stuffed the book under her pillow. Jon sat cross-legged on the bed next to her. They were both dressed for a banquet—Emily wearing a sea green, ruffled dress, and Jon looking like a little gentleman in a dark blue suit.

Emily shot up onto her knees and clutched the folds of her skirt, as if expecting criticism from Julie. Her eyes sparkled defiantly, though a trace of uncertainty lit their depths.

"Why, Emily!" Julie enthused with a smile. "Thank you for seeing to it that Jon dressed—and what lovely outfits you both have on. I always did enjoy dressing up as a child."

At the absence of ridicule, Emily's eyes widened in surprise. Jon's nose scrunched in distaste. "Don't want to be 'lovely,' " he mumbled, pulling off his clipped bow tie. "Lovely's for girls."

"Handsome," Julie corrected. "I meant you look handsome."

Jon beamed, though Julie noticed he didn't replace the tie.

Emily offered a tentative smile. "I like to pretend I'm a princess hidden away in a castle. Sometimes Jon is my knight who comes to save me, but most of the time he's just my brother the prince, and we're both locked away by the evil king and waiting to be found." The smile disappeared. She scooted off the bed and took the boy's hand. "Let's go, Jon."

Julie wondered as she stood and watched the small pair walk down the stairs, then hurriedly moved to join her charges. In the dining room Jonathan again pulled back his sleeve to glance at his watch. He looked at Julie but didn't say a word. In fact, throughout the meal silence reigned.

The children ate their food quietly and quickly. Their gazes barely lifted from their plates. Jonathan ate more slowly, his curious gaze repeatedly lighting on Julie.

Uneasy, Julie swallowed, forcing the curried fish past the block in her throat. She almost choked on the wild rice when Jonathan suddenly spoke and asked the maid to bring dessert, but a gulp of lemon tea saved her from complete disgrace. Was it always like this?

She looked away when his unnerving steel gray eyes met hers a fifth time over the table. Mrs. Leighton walked in with a dessert tray—four crystal dishes each loaded with peach cobbler and topped with a mound of vanilla ice cream.

"None for you, Jon. After that stunt you pulled today, you're to have no sweets for a week. You may go to your room now." Jonathan's voice seemed incredibly loud in the unnatural silence of the room.

"Yes, Daddy."

Julie watched the light go out of the child's eyes as he obediently left the table.

Emily threw her father a hard look, pushing away the dessert Mrs. Leighton had stiffly placed in front of her. "I'm not hungry. I'll go with Jon." She slid off her chair.

"Emily, I do not recall giving you permission to leave the

table. Sit down and finish your dessert," her father commanded. At the rebellious look suddenly sparking her eyes, his tone came more softly. "You know how you love peaches with ice cream."

The girl slid back on her seat but only picked up her spoon and toyed with her food. Though she didn't favor Jonathan in coloring, it was obvious to see she was her father's daughter. Every nuance of his expression was engrafted on the child's face—from the firm, set lips, to the high brow wrinkled in a frown, to the small chin tilted at a stubborn angle with slight evidence of a cleft in its middle. Even the aloof way she held herself reminded Julie of Jonathan.

A slam interrupted her perusal. Julie turned her head toward the kitchen door through which the housekeeper had just disappeared. Obviously the cantankerous woman wasn't in favor of the way Jonathan had dealt with his son either.

Julie's gaze went to the staircase just visible beyond the open doorway. She watched Jon's tiny figure trudge upstairs, his shoulders bowed.

"If you'll excuse me—" Julie pushed away her dessert. "It's been a long day."

Without waiting for Jonathan's permission she left the table, wondering if she too would be ordered back. When silence prevailed, Julie emitted a sigh of relief. She caught up with Jon and took his hand.

He looked up, teary-eyed. With a slight smile she squeezed his fingers, and together they went the rest of the way upstairs.

✦

Julie leaned her forehead against the cool pane in disappointment. Rain pounded the window, dropping the temperature by another ten degrees she was sure. Shivering, she pulled her cardigan from the desk chair, throwing it around her shoulders. If it was this cold now, how would she be able to stand the fall and winter, assuming of course she would still be here?

If she were to hold this job, she would have to manage better than yesterday. Imagine! First bounding downstairs—with all the aplomb of a boisterous teenager hearing the sound of a ringing phone—and running smack into her new employer, almost knocking him down. As if that weren't bad enough, forgetting to bring the children to dinner would surely put a splotch on her record, not even twenty-four hours old. Maybe her encounter with the icy Atlantic had frozen her brain?

Groaning, she shook her head. "Lord, please help me not to act like the incompetent fool Jonathan probably thinks I am by now," she murmured. "Give me Your grace to make it through this assignment—and any guidance You want to give concerning the children, I would really appreciate. I feel totally out of my element here."

Julie continued to stare out the rain-spattered window and wondered if the sun would make an appearance in a few hours. A bolt of lightning answered her unspoken question, followed by a deep rumble of thunder. Sighing, she turned away from the depressing view and studied the mint, blue, and cream room—the same room she was shown to after rescuing Jon.

She was accustomed to a jog in the predawn hours. A run in the cool air usually cleared the cobwebs from her mind and helped her think clearly. "Not that you'd know it from the way I've been acting," she muttered to the little blond girl who picked up shells in the seascape painting nearby.

Suddenly Julie felt a strong impression to check on Emily. She left her room and moved down the gloomy hall. Outside Emily's door she hesitated before turning the knob.

Moaning interspersed with soft, unintelligible words came from the slight figure writhing on the bed. Once Julie's eyes adjusted to the eerie darkness, she saw Emily twisted in the sheets, in the throes of a nightmare. Blue-white lightning illuminated the walls, followed by a sharp crack of thunder. The room returned to blackness.

Emily whimpered, and Julie went to her and turned on the

bedside lamp. "Emily?" She gently jostled her shoulder. "Emily, wake up. You're having a bad dream."

"Huh?" The child slowly came awake, her body trembling.

"Shh. It's okay." Julie drew the girl close and did the only thing she knew to do to alleviate any lingering fears. She sang a lullaby. The same one she had sung to Jon by the ocean. Minutes passed while she stroked Emily's silken locks, her soothing alto barely filtering over the sounds of the now-dying storm.

"No one's ever sung to me before."

Julie looked down into half-open eyes lazily observing her. "My momma sang that to me when I was a young girl," Julie said. "It's one of the nicest memories I have of her. She died when I was a little older than you are."

"My mommy died too." Emily seemed about to say something else then closed her mouth and looked away. "I want to go back to sleep now."

Julie released the child, disappointed that Emily had shut her out again. She rearranged the sheet and quilt over Emily's form then picked up the pillow, replacing it behind the child's head.

A sound on the other side of the partially open door, as though someone's shoe had bumped against the wooden frame, caused Julie to turn her head that way. Her heart lodged in her throat. Curious, she moved across the room and swung the door open. No one stood outside.

"Hello?" she whispered loudly, looking down both sides of the dark hall. "Is anyone there?"

Rapid muffled footsteps followed by the faint click of a door met her anxious query.

three

"What's wrong?"

Emily's worried voice alerted Julie before she could move to investigate. She turned her head to offer an encouraging smile. "Nothing's wrong. I thought I heard someone in the hall. Go to sleep. It's all right."

Julie left Emily's room, closing the door. She felt her way to her room to retrieve a slim pocket flashlight from her purse. On a whim she checked on Jon, whose room was between Julie's and Emily's. The boy slept soundly, his face turned toward the wall.

Julie shut Jon's door gently then moved in the direction of the other door she'd heard close. Someone had been spying on her and Emily, and Julie wanted to know who and why.

Four closed doors stood at that end of the hallway. She hesitated then cracked open the first to peek inside. A linen closet with floor-to-ceiling shelves filled the enclosed cubicle. She turned on the flashlight's narrow beam. No extra space where someone could hide. No tiny twin candlesticks engraved in the wood near hidden trapdoors.

Julie grinned wryly. She had cut her detection teeth on Nancy Drew and Trixie Belden mysteries and occasionally checked one out of the library to reread. Yet being a P.I. was worlds removed from the elaborate and fascinating mysteries Nancy and Trixie had solved. At least for Julie it was.

Opening the second door she discovered a bathroom with a window on the opposite wall. It had been left open a bit. Julie hurried inside, closing the door behind her. She moved to the window, lifted the pane all the way and looked down, shining her weak flashlight beam in the steady rain. As far as she could tell, there was no way down—no trellis, no ladder.

It was a long drop to the ground, but not a fatal fall for someone athletic, she supposed, and the soil was soft from the rain. Still, why would anyone escape out the window and into a thunderstorm?

Closing the window and exiting the bathroom, she moved toward the third door on the other side of the hall and put her hand on the knob. To her horror it moved before she could turn the handle. The door swung inward.

"Miss Rae?"

At the sound of Jonathan's gruff voice, she jumped, dropping her flashlight. Hastily she bent to retrieve it and straightened, lifting her gaze to his. He stood in the doorway, his hair tousled. In the dim lamplight coming from what was obviously his bedroom, she could see he wore a maroon terrycloth bathrobe that reached his knees. Awareness of his strong masculinity made her tighten her grip on the flashlight, but she couldn't think of a thing to say.

"I thought I heard someone lurking in the hall," he said, his brows raised in surprise. "It's four o'clock in the morning. Couldn't you sleep?"

She swallowed, wondering if he could hear the wild beating of her heart. "I–I was checking on the children."

His gaze dropped to her hand. "With a flashlight?"

"I don't know where the hall switch is for the overhead light. In fact, I still don't know the layout of many of the rooms," she added for good measure, glad she'd found her tongue again.

"Which would explain why you're at the wrong end of the hall," he said. "The children's rooms are that way, next to your room."

He moved forward, his arm sweeping upward to the side. Feeling as though her heart had leaped to her throat, Julie stepped back. His hand groped at the wall, and the hall came ablaze with light. "That's where the switch is located on this end. There's another switch on your end, next to Mrs. Leighton's room—which is opposite yours and down two doors."

"Thanks," she mumbled, flustered. "Oh, I never did ask—did the doctor's visit to Jon go well?"

"The doctor said Jon is fine." He looked at her a long moment, his expression unreadable. She wished she could discern his thoughts. "I'll ask Mrs. Leighton to give you a tour of the house after breakfast."

"I'd appreciate that." She took a faltering step backward. "Well, I'd best go to my room."

"Weren't you going to check on the children?"

"The children. Of course. I'll do that right now."

Aware of his steady gaze, Julie walked on shaky limbs to Jon's room. She put her hand to the knob and heard Jonathan's door click closed. Glancing over her shoulder, she saw no sign of him. Resting her forehead on the wood, she closed her eyes. The fourth door could wait. She didn't want to risk getting caught again.

❧

At her first opportunity, two days later, Julie investigated what lay beyond the fourth door. Mrs. Leighton hadn't included it and several other rooms on the tour, making Julie wonder. To her surprise the fourth door revealed a narrow staircase leading to the first floor. Taking it she found two doors—one leading to the kitchen and one leading outside. As old and large as the mansion was it must have been constructed with a separate staircase built for staff, to give them easier access to the house. Unfortunately it didn't make Julie's job any easier. Anyone could have been spying on her and Emily and escaped down that staircase. But who? And why?

"Miss Julie?"

Julie came back to the present and smiled at Jon, then surveyed the cards in her hand. "O–kaay—give me all your fives."

"Go fish." Jon giggled. As Julie retrieved a card from the deck on the floor between them, he asked, "Do you have any queens?"

"Not a one."

Jon drew from the pile and grinned. With a flourish he laid

his remaining cards in front of him. Julie looked at the two ladies smiling up at her then threw the five cards she held into the air. "Aggghhhh! You got me again." She clapped her hands to her chest, falling backward as if he'd shot her, and lay still upon the carpet.

Giggling at Julie's antics, Jon crawled over to her. A tickling match ensued but was soon interrupted by a hard voice.

"She let you win." Emily watched from across the room where she sat on a lattice-back rocking chair. "She could've beat you."

Jon sat up and stared at his sister. Raising his hand, he swiped at his dark hair, which had fallen into his eyes. Sadness filled them as he looked back and forth between Julie and Emily. It was obvious he believed everything his big sister said.

Julie eyed the girl. "Why do you say that?"

Emily flicked one blond braid over her shoulder, her green eyes steady. "Well, it's true, isn't it?"

"No. Jon won—fair and square. But why would you think I would let myself lose?"

The girl scoffed. "I know lots of times adults lie or pretend something is real, when it isn't. They think kids are stupid and don't know what's going on. But we do."

Julie felt Emily's words went a lot deeper than a mere card game. It was obvious the girl was hurting inside. Because of her mother's death?

Julie had noticed in the short time she'd been here how Emily distanced herself from adults, especially her father, and only seemed comfortable playing with Jon. Unobserved, Julie sometimes watched them together and had seen Emily laugh and play like a child her age should. But the minute she caught sight of Julie, all childishness evaporated to be replaced with indifference.

Such had been the case this afternoon when Julie stood at the door, watching the two play cards. Jon had caught sight of her and smiled, asking her to play with them. Immediately

Emily stood and walked to the chair in which she now sat, claiming she didn't want to play anymore. Puzzling Julie further was the fact that Emily never left the room but stayed close, her eyes keenly observing. If the girl despised Julie's presence as much as she implied, wouldn't she seek escape at every opportunity? Maybe Emily wasn't as indifferent to Julie as she pretended.

"Emily, you're right," Julie said, to the girl's evident surprise. "Sometimes adults don't tell the truth. Usually they're trying to protect children from hurt—they really do mean well. But I agree with you. I think it's wrong to lie. And I want you to know I would never lie to you or Jon about anything."

Emily narrowed her eyes, unbelief evident in the tilt of her chin, the crossed arms, the stiff shoulders. Her trust would obviously be a long time in coming, if Julie gained it at all.

Jon threw himself onto Julie's lap, a book in his hands. "Read to me!"

Julie smiled. Whether or not Jon understood all she'd said, she evidently had his trust. She reached for the book—almost dropping it when she saw a terrifying monster with yellow eyes and sharp pointed teeth leering at her from the cover.

She nudged Jon off her lap and stood, taking him by the hand and leading him to the waist-high, red wooden bookcase against one wall. "Let's see if we can't find something a little less scary, hmmm?" The story might not give the boy nightmares, but it would give them to her!

He studied the books, a serious frown wrinkling his brow, and pulled out another one. "How 'bout this?"

Julie looked at the title—*A Magical Day.* Four tiny fairies flitted through a lavender sky, holding their wands aloft and smiling at Julie, their eyes sparkling. "Ummm. No. I don't think so, Jon. Let's see what I can find."

Julie perused the shelves. Every book had to do with magic, witches, monsters, fairies, or other mythological creatures. She hardly considered this good reading material for impressionable young minds.

Suddenly she smiled. "I know! I'll tell you a story. How would you like to hear how a little boy—just like you—helped Jesus feed five thousand people?"

Jon's brow furrowed. "Who's Jesus?"

Shocked, Julie stared. "Why, He's the Son of God."

"Who's God?"

Julie was speechless. She glanced at Emily and saw the same question written in her eyes. Julie knew many in the world had never heard the gospel and didn't know there was a God. But she'd always assumed such people were in the jungles of Africa or in some other far-reaching wilderness. Not in the United States of America!

Julie released a long breath. "Maybe we'll save that story for another day. Let's talk about the day Jesus was born. Why do you think we have Christmas?"

"Santa Claus!" Jon piped up.

"Well, no—that's not the real reason," Julie said. "It's to celebrate the birth of Baby Jesus. Just like when you celebrate your birthday. That's why we give each other presents at Christmas. We're celebrating Jesus' birthday—so it's really like a big birthday party that everyone gets to take part in—"

"Is that why Santa brings us presents?" Jon interrupted, his brows drawing down in confusion. "I thought it was because we were good."

Oh, boy. This might take awhile. "Let me tell you a story that really happened long ago," Julie said. "One day a lady named Mary was visited by an angel—"

"What's an angel?"

Julie closed her eyes and prayed for guidance. It shouldn't surprise her that the boy didn't know the definition of an angel, since he'd never heard of God.

"An angel is a heavenly being who works for God and loves Him. Some angels are sent to protect us and keep us safe." Julie smiled. "I'm sure an angel kept you from drowning, Jon, until I could fish you out of the ocean."

His eyes narrowed in thought. "What do angels look like?

I didn't see anybody but you there."

"No, you usually can't see them, though some people have. I've heard they're strong and bright and beautiful, and some have wings and—"

"Like good fairies!" Emily broke in from across the room, evidently interested despite her desire to remain aloof. "We saw paper angels at the store two Christmases ago, Jon. Remember? They look like good fairies."

Good fairies? Julie's heart sank. This would take a great deal of patience and time, but she had that. Perhaps this was another reason God had brought her to this cold place. So that she could bring the warmth of His love into the lives of two small children.

Julie smiled at Emily. "There's a lot I'd like to share with you, with both of you. But for now let's talk about the true meaning of Christmas."

☙

Julie stood in front of the books gracing one entire wall of the room, examining the titles on the bindings. The children had long ago gone to bed, and, unable to sleep, Julie had stolen downstairs and into the library for a book to read.

Nothing appealed. She wanted light reading, but everything here looked either too deep or too gloomy. She was about to give up and turn away, when a surprised voice stopped her.

"Miss Rae—I didn't know you were still up."

Gathering her wits, she stared at the hardback binding of *Hamlet* a few seconds longer before turning to face her employer. "I was trying to find something to read to help me sleep," she admitted, feeling as if the walls had suddenly closed around her.

Jonathan stood on the inside of the door, his compelling gray eyes steeped in mystery. His strong presence seemed to overpower the room. The man was too mesmerizing for his own good. For her own good.

Jonathan walked closer, taking inventory of her appearance.

Julie cringed when she took mental note of what he saw. A gray sweatshirt over faded navy-blue sweatpants. She'd lost the sweatpants that matched the shirt years ago and only wore the ensemble for sleepwear now. Add to that her curls had declared mutiny—casting themselves in wild abandon over her head in a tangle with which a comb didn't have a chance. At least she was wearing a matching pair of socks tonight—even if they were covered with yellow smiley faces. She wished the bookcase would fall on top of her and put her out of her misery.

Flustered with the way he continued to stare, she blurted out, "Mrs. Leighton told me the library was open to the staff. Otherwise I wouldn't have come."

He nodded. "Perfectly all right. You're welcome to visit for reading material anytime." His gaze dropped to her feet, and a grin played on his lips. "Anytime," he repeated, his gaze rising to hers.

Nervous, Julie finger-combed her curls but stopped when she realized she was making them worse. Clearing her throat, she turned back to the case and reached for the first book her fingers touched.

"This will do," she said, pulling the thick volume out. She pivoted again, avoiding eye contact. "Well, I'll leave you to—whatever."

"Miss Rae?"

At his amused tone her gaze snapped his way.

He looked at the book she cradled against her chest. "I hardly think *The Complete Works of Edgar Allen Poe* will help you sleep. Of course everyone has their own ideas."

"Oh! Wrong book." Julie whirled and quickly crammed the volume back into position at the end of the shelf, her fingers sliding against the wood. Something pierced her finger above the knuckle, and she sharply inhaled through her teeth, making a hissing sound.

"Are you all right?"

Before she could answer, Jonathan took her by the shoulders, turning her toward him. He lifted her hand, inspecting it. Trembling, as much from his nearness as from embarrassment, Julie watched him pluck a wooden sliver from her skin.

"Thank you," she managed.

His enigmatic eyes met hers. "My pleasure. I'll see to having that sanded down. The bookcase is fairly old."

Words ceased as some invisible bond wrapped around them, drawing them close. The silence stretched and lengthened—until it was broken by the reverberating bongs of the grandfather clock in the hallway, striking the hour of twelve.

Jonathan blinked and released her hand, moving away. "I don't think I have anything that would help put you to sleep—unless you'd like to flip through the pages of my books on fish hatcheries, running a corporation, or business monopolies?"

His tongue-in-cheek question made Julie smile, and the atmosphere eased as the strange tension between them dissipated. "I'd heard you own Taylor Sardines. It's my favorite brand."

"Ah, a satisfied consumer." He grinned wryly. "Being the oldest son, my father's monopoly passed to me—including every single problem associated with the company."

"I take it you're not happy being the Taylor Sardine King?" She used the name dubbed him in an article she'd read about his inheriting the corporation.

"It's kept me away from home more often than I'd like, though since I've recently hired a capable manager I've had fewer problems. I'm also president of a small shipping industry, one I started seven years ago."

Julie nodded. The research Tina dug up on Jonathan had shown he was extremely wealthy. His assets were in the millions. Still, for all his money, Julie could tell he wasn't happy. Neither, it seemed, were his children.

"I understand your wife was your partner."

He jerked back in surprise. "In name only. Angela never had an interest in the business." A chill frosted his words.

An uneasy silence fell, and Julie felt it was time to make

her exit. "Well, those two will be up before you know it."
She lifted her little finger. "Thank you for this."

He nodded but didn't reply.

Once out of the room, Julie exhaled deeply, still shaken by
the encounter they'd shared, though she was sure she had suc-
cessfully kept that fact from him. Before the clock gonged,
she'd thought he would kiss her—and for a few crazy, mind-
numbing seconds she had wanted him to. What was wrong
with her?

Clutching the staircase rail, Julie tried to bundle her stray
thoughts into one neat package. She was here because
Jonathan Taylor was thought to have murdered his wife. She
was supposed to be collecting evidence pertaining to the case.
She could not—repeat, could not—afford any romantic
notions, however farfetched they may be. To let anything
cloud her judgment and keep her from remaining neutral was
dangerous to her job. She must keep herself at a distance. The
cool observer. The hired employee. The unflappable detective. Logic penetrated her brain and gained the upper hand as
she let herself into her room.

※

Several days later at breakfast, while the family sat around the
table eating pancakes drenched in maple syrup and butter,
Jonathan announced he was leaving that afternoon on business.

Julie put down her fork in surprise. "A business trip?"

He nodded. "Problems with Taylor Sardines. There's talk
of a strike among the workers. I need to be there."

The children continued to eat, barely flickering their eye-
lashes. Obviously they wouldn't miss their father. Or perhaps
they were accustomed to his frequent business trips?

Julie studied Jonathan's handsome features then looked
down at the syrup pooling over the stacked pancakes and onto
her plate. At least his absence would provide the opportunity
needed to proceed with her investigation, which had advanced
at a snail's pace. Besides a few subtle questions directed to the
children and three of the staff, Julie hadn't delved too deeply.

True, the children did take up a great deal of time, but Julie doubted they were the real deterrent to her work. Again her eyes flicked to Jonathan, and she knew the truth as suddenly as if someone had shouted it through a megaphone.

She didn't want Jonathan to be a murderer. If Julie began to uncover facts that pointed to that probability, she didn't want to face the truth. She promptly told herself the reasons for her unusual amount of concern were the children and the repercussions it would have on their young lives should their father be found guilty. She had grown to care deeply for little Jon and, yes, even the unapproachable Emily. With a pang of remorse Julie realized she had broken a major rule she'd set for herself in her line of work: Never become emotionally involved.

"Miss Rae, did you hear what I said?" Jonathan's deep voice intruded into her disturbing thoughts.

She looked up, startled, her hand still fingering her juice glass. "I'm sorry. No, I didn't."

He studied her, frowning. "At this point I'm not sure how long I'll be gone. I'll give you a number where I can be reached in case of an emergency."

"Oh—of course." She pasted a bright smile on her face. Did her voice sound a little too exuberant?

He gave her an odd look but said nothing more—much to Julie's relief. The rest of the meal passed in silence.

The morning sped away, and soon the time came for Jonathan to leave. Bag packed, wrapped in his raincoat, he stooped down and pulled Emily into his arms for a hug and a kiss. She went to him stiffly and pulled away at the first opportunity.

Hurting for both of them, Julie averted her gaze from the raw pain she saw in Jonathan's eyes at Emily's rebuff. Jon approached him hesitantly, almost as if he might change his mind, turn, and bolt from the room. Jonathan gave the boy a hug, but Julie noted it lacked the warmth of the one he'd given Emily. Why?

Good-byes said, the children raced upstairs to the playroom.

Jonathan straightened and stood in front of Julie. Their eyes met.

For a fleeting moment she found herself wanting to be on the receiving end of one of his hugs. Her cheeks grew warm, and she spoke to disguise her nervousness. "Don't worry. I'll take good care of them." Before she thought about what she was doing, she touched his arm. "God go with you and keep you safe."

He started in surprise, his gaze traveling to her slim hand resting lightly on his coat sleeve. He looked at her then. "Thank you, Miss Rae. But I doubt He'd want anything to do with a sinner like me." His low words were satiated with regret.

Shock swept his features when he realized what he'd said. Yet before Julie could blink, the familiar mask of indifference slammed across his face, shielding the glimpse of his soul she had just seen.

He said a gruff good-bye, snatched up his leather suitcase and briefcase, and made a hurried exit to the Rolls Royce waiting for him below.

Clutching the doorframe, Julie watched his departure. Her parting words and gesture had been an automatic action—a way she had bid her father good-bye in the past. But this had turned into more. Much more.

Her small action had been a catalyst, allowing her to see in a moment the deep suffering Jonathan was going through. She couldn't ignore or deny the look of condemnation and hopelessness she'd briefly seen in his tortured eyes. And his anguished words had sent a knife through her heart.

"Oh, dear God, no. Is he guilty?"

Her soft cry went unanswered. Julie closed the door, knowing what she must do. It was past time to dig for the truth of what happened there the night Angela drowned. And though she couldn't pray for God to change the past, whatever it revealed, she could pray for Jonathan's future and for the future of his children.

four

Julie made a circle with the red pen around a listed number. A few phone calls later she closed the phone book, satisfied. She turned to the housekeeper who had just entered the library with a duster in hand.

"Mrs. Leighton—I was just going in search of you."

The older woman grunted but said nothing. She swept her duster along the mantel.

"I'd like to arrange transportation to town in the morning for the children and me. Whom do I talk to?"

The housekeeper turned, frowning. "Mr. Taylor won't like it. He doesn't let the children go anywhere." A hint of disapproval tinged her voice.

"I'll take full responsibility. Now if you would be so kind as to tell me whom I need to talk to?"

Mrs. Leighton fixed her with a critical stare. "Clancy. He has a room over the garage."

"Thank you." Julie headed outside into the sunshine. Inhaling deeply, she smiled. What a wonderful change from the dreary weather they'd been having!

She found a tall man of slender build fiddling with various mechanisms under the open hood of a flashy red Corvette—hardly what she imagined the austere Jonathan Taylor would drive. Behind him in the long garage sat the silver-gray Rolls Royce Jonathan had ridden in to the airport and a dark blue Lincoln Town Car. Yes, that seemed more his speed.

At her approach the man straightened, his blue eyes widening. He swiped back a lock of blond hair with the back of his dirty arm. The motion left a streak of grease on his forehead, and Julie tried her best not to laugh at the ridiculous picture he made.

42

"I'm looking for someone named Clancy."

"Ron Clancy's the name. And to what do I owe this honor?"

"I need transportation into town tomorrow."

"For such a pretty lady I think I could spare the time."

His eyes roved her form, irritating Julie. She knew she was anything but pretty. "Athletic" and "sporty" were often used to describe her looks. "Home-girl fresh" and "cute" were the nicest compliments she'd ever received.

A cutting remark trembled on the tip of her tongue, but she managed a vague smile instead, reminding herself she was here to gather information—not to start a war. "If you have other duties, that's fine. I can drive."

He shrugged. "It's my job."

"Oh. Have you worked here long?"

"Three years."

"Then you were here when Mrs. Taylor died."

His eyes narrowed in suspicion, and Julie quickly looked down at the engine, deciding it best to switch the topic. "What a beautiful car. Is it yours?"

"Are you kidding? I could never afford this kind of luxury—not on my pay!"

"Surely this doesn't belong to Mr. Taylor? It doesn't look like something he would drive."

"It was Angela's—his wife. Now there was one classy lady. At least she saw to it that the old skinflint paid me more than I'm making now."

Julie made a mental note of his familiar use of Angela Taylor's first name. "She must have been nice."

"Nice? Yeah, you could say that. She treated me like I was somebody—not just a hired hand." He grew pensive. "She liked to take long drives along the coast in the Rolls. We'd be gone for hours, sometimes all day, and she'd leave the window between us open. We had a great time talking. At least we did until Mr. Taylor put a stop to those drives," he muttered. "Angela came to me in tears that day. It took some time to calm her down."

And I'm sure you enjoyed every minute of it, Julie thought wryly. She'd already pegged him as a wanna-be Casanova. "You two must have been close for her to come to you when she was upset."

A guarded look came into his eyes. "We were just friends."

"Of course. I didn't mean to imply—" Julie acted flustered. She shoved her hands into her jeans pockets. "I'm just beginning to realize how hard it will be to fill her shoes. I'm the children's new nanny."

"So—you're the one?" A gleam of interest sparked his eyes.

"Yes. And in the short time I've been here I realize what a task I've taken on. The children miss their mother a great deal. She must have loved them very much."

"Yeah, I guess. Wanna take in a movie some night?"

"No, thanks. Emily and Jon are a big responsibility, and I doubt I'll have much spare time. I don't see how Mrs. Taylor did it. Manage free time for rides in the country, I mean."

"Who—Angela? She always found time to have fun. Like a kid at Christmas—always smiling and laughing and finding excitement with everything she came in contact with. Never a dull moment with her."

"And was she happy with Mr. Taylor?"

"With him?" He scoffed. "Who could be happy with that brute? He killed her as sure as I'm standing here."

"Surely you don't know that for certain?"

"No. But the maid heard them fight the night Angela died. To hear her tell it, they were at each other's throats."

Dismay filled Julie. "You mean the housekeeper—Mrs. Leighton?"

"Naw—not ol' Eagle Eyes. Bessie Lou. Only she isn't here anymore. She got a job at the ice cream parlor in town."

"I see."

Clancy's eyes narrowed suspiciously. "Say—why do you care anyway? And why are you asking so many questions?"

"Isn't it only natural for me to be interested in the family I'm working for?"

"I guess," he said, his expression still uncertain. "A word of warning, though. Steer clear of Mr. Taylor. He's bad news."

"If he's so terrible, why do you stay? Why don't you find work somewhere else?"

He shrugged. "Jobs are hard to come by. I may not be making much, but at least I'm not out of work like my brother, Paul."

"I see. Well, I need to get back to the children before they wake up from their naps. Please be ready to leave at nine-thirty tomorrow."

"In the morning?" he asked incredulously.

"Yes. Church services start at ten."

"Church services?" A pained look crossed his face.

Julie raised her brows. "Didn't I tell you? I'm taking the children to church tomorrow. It's Sunday, you know."

"Sunday. Right." He stuck his greasy hands in his coveralls. "I just remembered. I can't make it—sorry. I promised Paul I'd come over and help fix his car."

"Oh." She smiled. "Well, I guess we'll have to manage on our own then." As she walked away, Julie could hear Clancy muttering under his breath about her being "one of those kind." Her thoughts trailed to their conversation, playing it back. It was time to seek out Bessie Lou. Julie wondered if Emily and Jon would enjoy an ice cream sundae after church.

❧

Julie steered the Lincoln into a parking space at the front of the wooden building with the steeple. She was glad to have found such a close spot, considering they were late because of Jon's missing shoe. "Okay—everyone out!"

Emily looked out the window. "Where are we?"

"Church."

"Church?" both children intoned, as if Julie had just offered them a plate heaped with green peas.

"Yeah, church." Peeking into the rearview mirror, she noticed the uncertain look that passed between them. "I thought afterward we could stop at the ice cream parlor for a sundae."

"Ice cream?" Jon asked, a hopeful smile on his face.

"But first—church."

The two looked at one another again, shrugged, and exited the car. As they walked to the entrance of the quaint building, Julie noticed Emily's hand going to the back of her hair to touch the green velvet bow fastened there.

Julie had offered to fix Emily's hair "up special" that morning and had been surprised when the girl allowed it. In place of the usual braids, sections of hair were gathered by the bow and fell down her back in rippling golden waves. Emily wore the same green, ruffled dress she'd worn the first night Julie had come to the Taylor home. The girl looked like a little princess, and Julie could tell Emily was pleased, though she'd offered Julie no more than a quiet thank-you.

Jon wore his blue suit and looked like a little gentleman. Even Julie had dressed for the occasion in a navy-colored linen dress sprinkled with tiny white flowers.

She ushered the children inside, where a kind-faced usher greeted them, handed them a bulletin, and seated them toward the middle. Julie began to worship with the others, as the congregation sang "We Exalt Thee." The children stood silent, looking around curiously, until the praise and worship ended and everyone took a seat. The message was inspiring, about trusting God to turn evil around to good. Only once did Julie have to correct Jon—when he picked up the bulletin, rolled it up and put it to his eye like a periscope, dropping his head far back and studying the beamed ceiling through his paper instrument.

After the service Pastor MacPhearson greeted Julie and the children, inviting them to join the others in a fellowship dinner.

"We can't," Julie replied. "But thanks for the invitation."

"We have a dinner once a month. You're always welcome."

"I'll take you up on it sometime." Julie smiled, firmly

holding on to the wrist of a writhing Jon. "You're Scottish, aren't you?"

He laughed, his eyes twinkling. "You'd think after spending fifteen years in Maine I would have lost the accent by now. But, yes, you guessed correctly. Ah, here's me bonny wife."

A little gray-haired woman with roses in her cheeks and a sparkle in her blue eyes came up to them. "Hello. I'm Agnes. And I'm so glad you came to visit with us today. You must stay for the meal. We have a bounty of food!"

"I'm sorry, but as I was just telling your husband, we can't. Maybe next time."

"Of course. I do hope we'll see you next Sunday, Mrs.—?"

"Rae. Julie Rae. And it's Miss," she corrected the woman with a smile.

"Oh. Of course." Julie saw the pastor and his wife glance at the children and then back at Julie with a guarded look.

She laughed. "Oh, no! You have it all wrong! This is Emily Taylor and her brother, Jon. I'm their new nanny."

"Did you say Taylor?" the pastor asked. "Then Jonathan is their father?"

Recognition tinged his voice, and Julie didn't think it was only because of what the media had written. She would have liked to pursue the conversation, but at that moment the usher walked up to the pastor, motioning him aside.

The pastor nodded at the usher's quiet words then turned back to Julie. "One of our members has just been taken to the hospital and is asking for me. I need to go, but I hope to visit with you again, Miss Rae."

"Of course. I look forward to it." Julie smiled through her frustration and watched him hurry away. If only she could have had a few more minutes with him.

❧

As they neared the ice cream parlor, Jon's voice broke into Julie's thoughts.

"Can I have something else instead of a sundae?"

"I don't see why not."

"Well, I want a sundae—a hot fudge one," Emily piped up.

Julie grinned and parked before the red and pink glass-encased building with gingerbread trim and a sign bearing the curlicue letters: The Sweet Eatery Pastry and Ice Cream Shoppe. The children were out of the car before Julie turned off the ignition. She locked the doors and hurried to follow them inside.

They claimed a booth near the wall. Jon was so excited he bounced on the red-cushioned seat. Emily looked around, her sparkling eyes absorbing everything, from the pictures of treats adorning the walls—hoping to tempt the customer's palate—to the ceiling fans making slow revolutions above them, to the cane chairs sitting at intimate round tables in the middle of the room. Suddenly her eyes widened, and her face paled.

Julie turned and saw a waitress bearing down on them, menus in hand. When she stopped at their table, Julie could see the nametag, which read "Bessie Lou."

"Well, looky who we have here—Jon and Emmie!" she exclaimed in a Southern drawl, very much out of place in Maine. "Well, well, well." Curious brown eyes lit on Julie. "And you are—?"

"The children's nanny," Julie inserted. She smiled at the brassy redhead. The cotton-candy pink uniform didn't do much for her, nor did the thick makeup, but her smile seemed genuine.

"What can I do for you folks?"

"We need a hot fudge sundae and one cup of hot cocoa—extra marshmallows. Jon is still deciding, I think." She looked at the boy who studied first the menu then the photographs on the wall.

Emily shook her head. "I'm not hungry anymore."

Julie noticed she hadn't looked in Bessie Lou's direction once since the waitress had come to their table.

"I want one of those!" Jon exclaimed, pointing to the wall behind Julie.

Julie turned and saw a picture of a huge concoction made

with mounds of flavored ice cream dripping with chocolate sauce, huge chunks of fudge pieces, white chocolate shavings, nuts, and heaps of whipped cream with a few cherries sprinkled on top. It was appropriately labeled "The Himalayan Avalanche."

"Uh, I don't think so, Jon. That looks like too much—even for a big boy like you."

"It doesn't look so big."

Julie sighed and turned to the waitress. "Make that one hot cocoa and one of those—but bring two spoons. I think he might need help with it."

Bessie Lou winked. "Gotcha. Back in a flash."

When the huge dish arrived and was set before Jon, his eyes widened in anticipation. Quickly he picked up his spoon and dove in. Emily licked her lips as she watched him shovel a heaping bite into his mouth.

"Jon, why don't you and Emily share that?"

"Sure," he said around a mouthful of ice cream. He slid the platter closer to his sister, and soon they were both immersed in the rich, gooey treat. Julie took several sips of her hot cocoa and watched them. She felt sorry for the two, cooped up in that house all the time and never getting to go places, like the ice cream parlor. What was Mr. Taylor thinking to enforce such a rule?

Seeing that the children would be occupied for some time, Julie rose from the table. "I'll be right back, kids. I'm going to pay the bill."

They barely acknowledged her as they spooned the thick dessert down their throats at an alarming rate.

At the counter an older woman took Julie's money. Bessie Lou was nowhere in sight. "Excuse me? Where's the ladies' room?" Julie asked.

"Behind the jukebox, down the hall and to your right."

"Thanks. Mind keeping an eye on those two while I'm gone?"

The woman looked at the children engrossed in their confection and nodded. "Sure. We're not all that busy right now."

Julie thanked her and went in search of Bessie Lou. At the rate those two were eating, she didn't have much time. As Julie opened the door, she saw her efforts were rewarded.

Bessie Lou stood next to the stalls, primping in front of the mirror. When she saw Julie, she stopped, her eyes brimming with curiosity. "I must say, I'm plumb surprised to see Mr. Taylor let those two come to town."

Julie smiled. "You seem to know the children well."

"I should say so! I worked at the Taylor home for a spell."

"Really? Then perhaps you could tell me a little about what to expect. I mean—I haven't worked there long, and I don't want to make any mistakes," Julie explained.

The redhead frowned. "You're asking the wrong person. Mr. Taylor fired me."

"Oh," Julie said, with just enough inflection in her voice to encourage Bessie Lou to continue.

"His wife was murdered, and I happened to have some important information to tell at the hearing," she bragged, leaning against the counter and crossing her arms, obviously happy to have a listening ear. "You see—it was Mr. Taylor who done it. But after he was ex—ex—"

"Exonerated?"

"Yeah! That's the word they used. Anyway, after he was exonerated, he fired me."

"I had heard something about his wife's death. But surely if he was exonerated—which, by the way, means he was freed from blame—then there wasn't enough evidence to suggest he had done such a thing. So why do you feel he was guilty?"

"I heard them fighting the night she drowned. A storm was brewing, and everyone in the house was edgy. You could feel it in the air. Ya know what I mean?"

Julie nodded.

"Well, Mrs. Leighton was mad at me for some dusting I hadn't done, and she ordered me downstairs to do it, even though it was late—I always thought the old bat senile. Well, the room was right next to the one that Mr. and Mrs. Taylor were in, and they had left the door cracked so I could hear 'most every word he said—or yelled, I should say. I'd never heard him blow his cool like that. Usually when he got mad, he was just kind of quiet-mad. Ya know what I mean?"

"Yes. What exactly did he say?"

"It didn't make much sense—I didn't hear the beginning of the fight. But he was accusing her of going out with someone, and I heard him yell something about the kids. He was pretty mad, so he wasn't real clear. Ya know?"

Julie nodded, and Bessie Lou continued. "Well, her voice got real quiet-like. All I could hear was a lot of mumbling. And then she laughed. He began calling her all kinds of terrible names, and she said something back, though I couldn't hear what. She didn't yell like he did, so I didn't hear a lot of what she said—but I heard her cry a lot after that. And I heard what he yelled at the end, 'cause by that time I'd gotten close enough to hear better.

"He told her, 'You don't deserve the children, and you're not fit to live another day on this earth.' Then he called her another nasty name. She said something back, and I heard a loud slap. I think he's the one who did it 'cause she cried out. Then I heard her running away and a door slam, and I heard him go after her and the door slam again."

With each word Bessie Lou spoke, Julie's heart grew heavier. "I'm surprised the charges were dropped—especially if you were a witness."

Bessie Lou straightened from the counter and smoothed her shirt-dress. "Aw. He's got a hotshot lawyer—one of the best money can buy. When you've got money, you can buy anything, I reckon. Even freedom."

Julie turned on the cold water and washed her hands. Bessie Lou might grow suspicious if she didn't do something while she was there, and she didn't want her to blab it around town that the new Taylor governess had sought her out asking questions. Judging from Bessie Lou's personality, Julie knew a great deal of what the woman said was probably pure gossip—something Julie didn't care for. Yet in her line of work it was necessary to listen with an open mind and weed out truth from hearsay. That's why concrete proof was so important. And it was Julie's job to find it.

"It was nice talking to you, Bessie Lou. Thanks for the info. I'll be sure to watch myself." Julie pressed the button of the hand dryer and put her hands under the hot air.

"Just don't go making Mr. Taylor mad. There's no telling what he might do. In fact, if I was you I'd high-tail it out of there before something happens."

Julie turned a thoughtful gaze the woman's way. "I'm curious. Why did you stick around if you thought it dangerous to work there? Why didn't you quit directly after Mrs. Taylor's death? I understand the hearing was held weeks later."

She shrugged. "I was sure he'd be found guilty. But I wouldn't have stayed on with him around anyway, even if I hadn't testified and he hadn't fired me—not after what happened to her. He might've murdered me too."

"Oh." Julie noted Bessie Lou's cheeks had reddened, making her face look splotchy, and her eyes had flitted away from Julie's direct stare. Something more was going on here. Just what was Bessie Lou hiding? "I'll give some thought to what you said. I've got to get back to the children now."

Bessie Lou glanced at her gold wristwatch. "And I'd better get back out there before Maude comes looking for me."

Before Julie could leave, Bessie Lou grabbed her arm. "Just be careful. I think Jonathan Taylor must be a crazed lunatic."

five

Julie pulled the car into the garage, parking it next to Angela's Corvette. Fortunately she saw no sign of Clancy.

No sound had issued from the backseat for the past ten minutes, and she looked over her shoulder. Both children looked terrible, their faces drawn, their eyes half-closed.

"What's wrong?"

"I don't feel good, Miss Julie."

"Me either."

Instantly Julie was worried. "I hope there isn't a bug going around. Let's get you both inside and into bed."

They moaned as they straightened from their bent positions and followed her to the house, arms clasped about their stomachs. As they neared the kitchen, Mrs. Leighton came out to greet them.

"There you are," she said to the children. "I've made your favorite for brunch—blueberry and banana pancakes with fresh strawberries on the side." She smiled, her gaze softening, obviously sure of an ecstatic reply.

"I think I'm going to be sick." Emily clapped a hand over her mouth and ran from the room. Jon looked a little green. He didn't follow, but his eyes clearly showed his misery.

"What's wrong with her? You don't look too good either, Jon—and what did you get on your shirt?" Mrs. Leighton rubbed her thumb and finger over a brown stain on his collar. "How did this happen? Did you get into some mud?"

The boy shook his head but didn't say anything.

"I believe that's fudge sauce," Julie offered.

"Fudge sauce?"

"I took them to the ice cream parlor after church."

Mrs. Leighton looked down her nose at Julie, as if she

were an insignificant insect. Julie squirmed, suddenly feeling very much like one of the specimens in Jon's bug keeper.

"And what did they have for breakfast?" the housekeeper asked, her tone icy.

"Breakfast?"

The woman's eyes widened. "Are you telling me you let the children leave this house without eating breakfast first?"

"No, no—of course not," Julie replied. "Let's see—they each had two pieces of buttered toast with jam and a glass of juice."

"And that's all?"

Julie nodded sheepishly. That was all she usually had when she fended for herself—and, of course, coffee. She'd been told that Mrs. Ruggles, the cook, took Sundays off and that she would be expected to prepare the children's breakfast. But Julie knew nothing about caring for the nutritional needs of children—she didn't even know how to cook. She'd had no one to teach her the art of homemaking.

"The poor dears—sundaes on an empty stomach." Mrs. Leighton clucked her tongue.

"Well," Julie added sheepishly, "actually it was more than a sundae—"

Mrs. Leighton flung her hands up to stop Julie's words. "I don't want to know—I don't think I could stand it. Get Jon into bed, and I'll fix them both something for their tummy-aches."

Feeling incompetent, Julie took Jon's hand. Upstairs in his room she helped him change into pajamas and tucked him in bed. "Sorry, Tiger. Guess I should've known better—me being an adult and all."

"That's okay, Miss Julie." He winced and curled his body into an embryonic position, making Julie feel even worse.

She suddenly noted that Mrs. Leighton stood at the door, glaring at her, a glass of something fizzy in her hand. "This will help him feel better," the housekeeper said. Though she didn't come out and accuse Julie of being irresponsible, the flashing eyes behind her spectacles did a good enough job of it. "I'll take over from this point on, if you don't mind. I know how to deal with a bad case of stomachache."

Julie cringed under the scorching heat of the woman's low words. "Of course."

Mrs. Leighton walked into the room and gave the glass to Jon. He wrinkled his nose at the smell and taste but drank every drop and lay back down.

"How's Emily?" Julie asked as she followed the housekeeper from the room.

"The same."

Uncomfortable silence followed.

"Well, if you're sure you won't need me, I think I'll change and take a walk," Julie said at last. "I know they're in good hands."

Narrowing her eyes, the woman gave a curt nod, and Julie headed to her room. Now was definitely not the time to interrogate the housekeeper.

Julie divested herself of her dress and pulled on a pair of jeans and a cable sweater in a sunny shade of yellow. Noticing the appearance of gray clouds in the east, she grabbed her windbreaker and headed out the door.

The wind had picked up, and it playfully whirled Julie's curls about her head. Hands in her jacket pockets, she walked along the path, her gaze frequently going to the small islands dotting the ocean in the distance.

Julie continued her walk until the mansion resembled a dollhouse in size. She harbored a strong desire to free herself from its burdens; yet she felt as though an invisible bond connected her to it—like a ball and chain. No matter how hard she tried not to think about Jonathan, the children, and their untold secrets, it was all her brain seemed able to come up with at the moment. Sometimes she hated being a detective.

She climbed up onto a short outcropping of rock. Pulling her knees to her chin, she clasped her arms about her lower legs and stared out to sea. Her mind churned as violently as the waves foaming on the rocks below her.

"Surely it can't be all that bad."

Startled, she turned to see who had spoken. A man, probably in his mid-thirties like Jonathan, stood a few feet behind her, a boyish grin on his face. Long reddish-blond strands of hair, loosened from his ponytail, blew around his head. Bright blue eyes, full of mischief and fun, regarded her. He seemed familiar, but for the life of her she couldn't figure out why.

His gaze went out to the ocean. "We're in for quite a storm, I'm thinking." His words had a faint lilt to them.

"Yes, a storm," Julie replied idly, her mind still trying to puzzle him out. "Do I know you? Have we met somewhere before?"

He turned back to her. "I believe that's supposed to be my line."

Julie's face grew hot at his implication that she was trying to flirt with him. "No—really. You seem familiar."

"I doubt I would have forgotten a pretty face," he said. Julie wryly raised her brows at the obvious line. He laughed. "I've just returned from being at sea for several months. Unless you've recently visited the continent of South America, I think you must be mistaken. We've never met. But I would be more than happy to remedy the situation. My name is Sean MacPhearson. Sean to my friends—'Fiery MacPhearson' to my enemies. I hope you will call me Sean." He delivered his words with a twinkle lighting his eyes.

"Of course!" Julie exclaimed. "Now I know why you look so familiar. Pastor MacPhearson must be your father."

His brows drew down. "Aye, that he is. Though I ken he would be likin' to forget it." His Scottish burr thickened dramatically. "I'm what is known as the black sheep of the family." Suddenly he laughed, erasing the serious lines in his bronzed face. "But I shouldna' be tellin' you that. Not when I was plannin' to ask if you'd care to walk with me. I wouldna' be wantin' to scare you away."

Julie studied him. Though he was big and brawny, something about him put her at ease. He had a certain boyishness about him that made her sure he wouldn't harm a fly, much less a person. "I'm not easily frightened," she said.

He held out his hand. She took it, sliding down to the ground beside him. He was tall—taller than Jonathan—and towered over her small stature. She retreated a step.

Amusement lit his eyes. "You seem too real to be a sea nymph the waters have coughed up onto the rocks. Have you a name?"

She smiled, his teasing words again putting her at ease. Together they began walking in the direction of the house. "It's Julie. Julie Rae."

"And where do you come from, Julie Rae?"

"I'm playing nanny to a pair of children who live here. But my actual home is in Florida."

"Ah, Florida. Where the sun always shines."

She smiled. "We see our share of rain too."

"But I'm willing to bet you see more sun than we do. This year especially it seems as if it's done nothing but rain."

Julie thought back to the past days of bad weather. "You don't sound as if you like it here much."

Sean shrugged and looked out to sea. "I'm a wanderer. No place is really home. But for some reason I always find myself drawn back here, though I don't want to be. It's almost as if invisible cords are drawing me to Breakers Cove. No matter how far I go, I have this strange desire to come back—but then, after a few weeks or months, I leave again for the secrets the sea holds. It's a continuous cycle." His gaze flickered to hers. "I imagine that sounds strange. Getting worried yet?"

"No. You seem sane enough. I'm sure what you're feeling is probably connected with your family being here. Family ties can be strong."

He gave a derisive laugh, shocking her. "Maybe in some families, but not mine. I have a feeling my parents cringe every time they hear I've returned from being at sea."

Julie stopped and faced him. "Oh, but I'm sure you're

wrong! I've met your parents, and they're some of the sweetest people on this earth."

"I see you've become a member of their fan club," he remarked dryly. "Which must mean you fit into their mold. I, on the other hand, don't."

"Their mold?"

"Christianity."

"Oh."

"It's not that I don't believe in God," he inserted, obviously aware of her silent withdrawal. "I just don't feel it's necessary to do things their way."

"And what's your way?"

Her question startled him. He obviously wasn't expecting it. "Well, for instance, God gave us a brain, and I believe He expects us to use it, to figure things out for ourselves."

"I agree."

"You do?" he exclaimed, a note of surprise in his voice.

"Of course. But He expects us to use our brains to read the Word and learn His ways. And, yes, He wants us to think things out—otherwise how can we make choices? But we have to have all the information first. The Bible is like a manual to help us." She glanced at him. "God gave mankind the gift of free will—it's true. But when we choose to do our own thing, we usually end up getting in trouble."

Sean was silent. Julie looked up into the lead gray sky. A white seagull tried to fly against the strong wind tossing him farther backward, making his progress slow. She pointed to the bird, gaining Sean's attention.

"Do you see that seagull? Our lives are like that. When we fight God and try to do our own thing, we have trouble going forward. Now if that seagull would turn and fly with the wind flow, his flight would be much easier and faster."

"But he'd be going in the opposite direction from what he wanted." His gaze met hers, his tone almost defiant.

"Yes, that's true. But maybe the way he was going was the wrong way in the first place," she countered softly.

His eyes widened; then he gave an easy laugh, and the serious moment disappeared. "You're quite something, Julie Rae. If my father ever needs a stand-in at the pulpit, you would fit the space nicely."

Her face grew hot. "Sorry. I didn't mean to sound preachy."

"Yes, you did."

Surprised at his amused words, a smile tugged at her lips. "Yeah, I guess you're right. Maybe I did."

Again he laughed. "I think I should like very much to know you better. As my father would say—you're a bonny wee lass."

They strolled along the path and soon came near the house. "This is where I'm staying," Julie said when he would have gone farther.

Sean looked up the cliff, startled. Did Julie imagine it, or did he stiffen? His once lively eyes were now shuttered and cold as he studied the house.

"Sean?"

Her small voice could barely be heard above the wind, but it snapped him out of his reverie. He gave her a smile with little warmth behind it. "It was a pleasure to meet you, Julie Rae. I hope we'll see each other again soon."

Too stunned to move, she watched as he turned and walked away. What had changed him so suddenly? He had turned from the companionable, easy-going man she'd met to a different person altogether. Bitterness had filled every line of his face, and his eyes had kindled with anger. Why?

She made her way up the footpath. Huge raindrops began to plop in dark wet patches on the ground around her, and she picked up her pace. The sparse shower soon became a monstrous torrent that drenched Julie before she made it to the door.

❧

"Bud I don'd wand do ged up." Julie moaned. "I juzd wand do sday here." But Shannon, the new hired help, wouldn't listen. Julie turned her face into her pillow. How could a little rain make her as sick as this?

"Mrs. Leighton said I was to run you a hot bath and make you get into it. And I wouldn't dare go against her orders," Shannon declared. Her shoulder-length spiral curls swayed as she shook her head. "That's how that last girl got fired. And I just got this job."

"Please. I juzd wand do sleep. I won'd tell." But Julie's pleadings went unheard as Shannon pulled her arm, forcing her out of bed.

Julie broke away from the new maid and walked into the bathroom, locking the door behind her. She laid her forehead against the door. The humidity in the room felt nice against her chilled skin. Maybe a hot bath wouldn't be so bad. She disrobed and stepped into the tub. Some kind of herbs had been sprinkled in the water, and Julie could feel the congestion begin to clear. She closed her eyes. Ahhhh, this was nice.

A pounding on the door awakened her. She jumped, splashing water onto the tiled floor.

"Better come and eat your chicken soup while it's hot," Shannon called. "I have to get back downstairs."

Julie sighed and pushed down the plunger to the drain. After drying off, she slipped into her robe and eased between the cool sheets, which she noticed had been changed. A tray sat nearby, a huge mug of steaming soup and a small plate of saltine crackers waiting. She pulled the covers up and reached for the meal. Halfway through the soup, she felt eyes upon her and turned, spotting Jon peering around the side of the door.

"Jon?" He darted away. "Id'z okay, Honey. Come in."

Jon's face appeared, followed by his body. "Mrs. Leighton said I should leave you alone."

"No. No. Id'z okay. I'd like the compandy," Julie told him. "Take a seat. Juzd don'd get too close. I don'd wand you catching thiz." She motioned to the foot of the bed.

It didn't take a second invitation for him to run to her mattress and plunk down on top of it. "When will you be all well, Miss Julie? It's no fun without you."

She smiled. "I'm sure I'll be feeling bedder soon. The fever broke thiz mornding. Id'z juzd my ndose ndow."

After some prodding on Julie's part, Jon told her about his past two days. Julie sneezed several times in succession, plucking several tissues from a nearby box.

Shannon came back in. "There you are." She shook her finger at Jon. "Your father's looking for you, young man."

"Mizdur Daylor is here?" Julie croaked, feeling as if the fever had suddenly returned. At least that would explain why her face grew so hot and she felt woozy.

In answer to her question his commanding form appeared in the doorway. Shannon offered him an uncertain smile then scurried out. Jon looked toward the door, and Julie noticed the half-hopeful look in his gaze. "Hi, Daddy."

Pain clouded Jonathan's eyes but was gone so quickly that Julie wondered if she'd imagined it. "Hello, Jon. Have you been good?"

"Yes, Daddy. Just ask Julie."

"I intend to. You go on and join your sister now. Dinner is in half an hour."

Jon slid off the bed. Only Julie saw the hope that had flickered in his eyes die out. Her heart ached for the little boy who so badly wanted his father's affection. After he left, an uncomfortable silence entered the room. At last Jonathan spoke. "Did he give you any trouble?"

"He was as good as gode," Julie defended him stoutly.

"You sound funny."

"I hab a code."

"Obviously." He was quiet a moment. "You look like a little girl all swallowed up in that huge blue robe."

Her cheeks flamed. "Id was my father's."

He continued to look at her, his gaze lifting to her damp curls. "Why is your hair wet? It's not wise to wash your hair when you're sick."

She bristled at this. "I fell asleep ind duh bathdub."

"Not too smart. You should be more careful." Her eyes narrowed, but he'd already looked away. "Well, when you're feeling better, I'd like to talk to you."

"Somethingk I'be done?"

He faced her again, a smile quirking the corners of his mouth. "You know, you sound cute when you talk like that."

"Then I'll be sure do ged a code more ofden so I can enderdain you."

"Sarcasm, Miss Rae? Somehow that doesn't fit the picture I have of you."

"And juzd whad picdure do you hab ub me, ib you don'd mind my askingk?"

"Not at all." He covered the distance to the foot of her bed. "I see a little girl still wet behind the ears, trying to play grown-up and failing miserably." He chuckled when she glared at him. "Good night, Miss Rae. Better finish your soup before it grows cold," he taunted as he left the room.

Julie slammed the tray onto the carpet, angry with the insufferable Jonathan Taylor, with the whole situation. She wondered what he would do if he knew who she really was and the reason she was under his roof. That would wipe the smirk off his face. Little girl—really!

Her mind zoomed back to the night in the library like a rewind button on a VCR. Jonathan certainly hadn't thought she was too young then. Not judging by the way he'd looked at her, as though he would kiss her.

Frustrated with her brain for its determination to play back that night, she burrowed her head into the pillow, hoping to smother such thoughts. The strange parting on the day Jonathan left for his business trip and his tortured words to her came to mind. She sat up and blinked.

Was he deliberately antagonizing her, hoping to put up a wall between them? She had seen his shock when he realized he'd allowed her to witness a buried piece of himself during their good-bye that day—or had one of the staff told him she'd been asking a lot of questions? Maybe he was worried she would find out too much. And that if he made her angry enough, she would drop any desire to continue—and perhaps even quit her job. The more she thought on it, the more reasonable it sounded.

"Well, Mizdur Jondathan Daylor. Hab you god a subrise comingk your way," she announced to the empty room. "I'm not easily intimbidated, as you'll soon discubber." Feeling better, she picked up her soup mug and finished the cooling liquid.

six

Julie only got halfway through the first chapter of the best-selling mystery before she slammed it shut, disgusted. This book with its plethora of four-letter words definitely didn't fit her idea of good reading material. She looked up and out the window. The day was sunny, beautiful, and she felt strong enough for a walk. Emily was drawing in her room, Jon was asleep, and Julie was about to go stir-crazy from the three days she had been cooped up in bed.

Jonathan strode into the library and stopped, looking as surprised to see her as she was to see him. As usual he looked like the definition of the word sophisticate, wearing a blue-gray cashmere sweater with black slacks.

"Feeling better?" he asked politely.

"Much, thank you. I thought I might go for a walk."

"You certainly sound improved." He studied her in amusement and lifted his brow. "Tell me—were you planning to go in your pajamas? All you need to complete the picture is your teddy bear."

Julie glanced at her rose-pink sweatshirt and pants. At least she didn't have on smiley socks this time. *I will keep my cool. I'm onto your game, Jonathan Taylor, and I think you'll find me a worthy opponent.*

"If my appearance bothers you, I don't mind changing. I need to talk to you about the children and would appreciate it if you'd join me." She flashed him a sweet smile, causing his own smile to waver. "In fact, I seem to remember you said you wanted to talk to me too."

"We can talk here," he said gruffly.

"I've been cooped up in this house for days. I need fresh air. It helps me think clearly."

"I'll open a window."

"No, I really need the exercise. I won't be but a moment," she assured him, hurrying from the room. A little over five minutes later she reentered the library. "Okay, I'm ready."

Turning to face her, he stared. Julie smothered a satisfied grin. Good. Now maybe he would stop with the little-girl jokes.

A soft white top, rimmed with pastel embroidered roses, gently outlined every curve and was tucked into a pair of slim-fitting jeans that showed off her slender waist. A dash of rosy lipstick glistened on her lips, and she'd combed her curls until they shimmered.

"I couldn't find my teddy bear," she said innocently, "so I opted for this instead."

His mouth tightened. In a few strides he was out of the library door and moving toward the hall closet. Once there he snatched her windbreaker from its hanger and tossed it to her as she approached. "You'll need this. It's cold."

She barely caught the jacket before it hit the floor. "Surely it can't be that cold. The sun is shining."

"Things aren't always as they seem, Miss Rae. You'd do well to remember that."

Julie relented. Maybe it hadn't been such a good idea to provoke him. "Okay, I'll wear it. Shall we go?" she asked with a penitent smile.

He gave a curt nod and moved with her toward the door.

Outside, a cool wind nipped her face, and Julie was thankful for the added warmth of the jacket. Jonathan seemed intent on making this outing into a foot race. At least that's what Julie surmised as he steadily kept a few paces ahead of her. A few yards farther down the path, he whipped around to stare.

"Well?" he asked with a frown. "I thought you wanted to talk about the children."

Julie halted and put her hands on her hips. "I do—but I'm not in the habit of yelling at someone's back!"

"Then why don't you keep up?"

"In case you haven't noticed, Mr. Taylor, my legs are shorter than yours. So why don't you slow down?"

Jonathan closed his eyes in an obvious fight for self-control. "All right, Miss Rae, you have my undivided attention. I will even resort to walking at a turtle's pace—though I thought you runners were supposed to move faster."

"When I run, I run. Right now I choose to walk."

"Okay, okay." He blew out an exasperated breath and adjusted his stride to hers. "So what's the problem? Jon's not giving you a hard time, I hope."

Julie stuffed her hands in her windbreaker pockets and clenched them. Why was he always so hard on his son? "Jon's an angel. Though a few things worry me about him. Emily too."

"Emily?" He stopped, and so did she. "What about Emily?"

"She has nightmares."

He studied her a moment then resumed walking. "All children have nightmares."

"She has them almost every night." Julie ran a few steps to catch up, glancing sideways at him. A nerve ticked in his cheek, and his expression was grim. "They're about her mother," Julie added when he didn't say anything. "And the night she died."

His pace increased, until Julie was once again running to keep up. "Mr. Taylor! Wait! We need to talk, and I—"

Jonathan stopped and whirled around, grabbing her shoulders when she almost ran into him. His fingers increased their pressure, and she winced.

"Tell me what you've heard," he ordered.

Confused, Julie shook her head. "What do you mean?"

"In a town this size, you're bound to have heard something by now. I know all about your Sunday outing. So tell me!"

Julie hesitated, wondering how much she should reveal. "I know her mother—your wife—drowned over a year ago."

White patches showed about his mouth. "And?"

"And there seems to be some kind of mystery about the whole thing."

He snorted. "Go on."

Staring into his stormy gray eyes, Julie tensed, preparing for his reaction to her next words. "Everyone says you're responsible. That you killed your wife."

Jonathan dropped his hold on her and turned away, facing the sea. His stance was as striking and sinister as the jagged boulders that lined the coast. Water splashing against the rocks was the only sound heard for a time. From out of nowhere, a great blue heron made a lightning dive toward the water and grasped a silvery fish in its long, sharp beak before flying away.

"I'll give you two weeks' severance pay." Jonathan's sudden emotionless words cut through the air.

Alarmed, Julie stared at his back. "You're firing me?"

He pivoted, his expression incredulous. "Surely you wouldn't want to stay in the house of a suspected murderer?" His tone was mocking.

"I told you what I heard. Not what I believed."

Hope sparked in his eyes, and the hard planes of his face softened. "And what do you believe?" he asked quietly.

Shaken, her heart missing a beat, Julie broke eye contact and stared at the sea's white froth on the rocks below. "Not hearsay, that's for sure. Give me some credit for having the intelligence to make my own decisions." She hesitated. "But, in making a decision, it's helpful to know both sides—"

Gathering courage, she looked at him. "I'm going to ask you this only once, and I'd appreciate an honest answer." She took a deep breath. "Were you in any way responsible for your wife's death?"

Her whisper-soft words charged the air like the aftermath of a dangerous explosion. Seconds of uneasy silence between them ticked by, until a seagull's sudden loud screeching came close to making Julie lose her footing and plummet over the cliff's edge. She moved a couple of feet sideways, away from the rocks, to a safer place on the path.

Jonathan's eyes narrowed. "Even if I were, what makes you think I'd confide in you? Can you give me one good reason why I should?" His tone sounded almost challenging, as though he were expecting something from her.

Julie hesitated. "You don't have to tell me a thing. Either way I choose to remain here and care for the children."

"Why?"

"For now let's just say it's because I feel they need me. And they need you too. Especially Jon. He craves your approval and needs you to spend time with him."

"I can't help that. I'm a busy man." He made as if to walk on.

"Then I guess that's that. Forgive me for taking up your valuable time." Irritated with his thick-headedness, Julie turned and began walking back to the house. She had gone only about ten yards when Jonathan's deep voice reached her ears.

"Wait."

Halting on the path, she heard his footsteps come up behind her and stop.

"I did not put a hole in that boat," he said, his words slow and steady. "I did not kill my wife."

Julie turned and searched his open gaze, looking into the very depths of his soul. Distress, pain, and unhappiness dwelt there. Yet so did honesty and hope.

"I believe you," she murmured.

His eyes widened, as though he wasn't sure whether to trust her statement or not. "Thank you," he said at last, his voice husky. He continued to stare. His hand lifted to her cheek, and his rough knuckles brushed her skin, sending her heart into spasms.

Julie felt as though she were being sucked into something over which she had no control. Powerless to resist, all she could do was watch him. The awed confusion in his eyes matched the way she felt. Time slowed as Jonathan lowered his mouth to hers.

The pounding surf seemed to have taken residence inside Julie's head, blotting out all other sound. The taste of salt on Jonathan's lips and the smell of his lime cologne intoxicated her senses, making her dizzy. She wrapped her arms around his neck to hold on, but also to draw him closer.

"Daddy!"

The wind carried Emily's hurt voice to them. Instantly Jonathan moved away, and they both looked to where the little girl stood on the footpath, less than fifty feet from them. She whirled and sped to the house. Mrs. Leighton stood at the door.

"I'd better go see what the problem is," Jonathan said, darting Julie a short glance before leaving.

Confused, Julie stared after him then turned and resumed walking in the direction they'd been going. She put her fingers to her trembling lips, which were still warm from Jonathan's kiss. Believing Jonathan innocent was one thing. But to accept his advances when the last thing she needed— or wanted—was to get involved in a relationship with him? That was pure idiocy.

Julie began to run, needing the release. The wind whipped through her short curls. She steadily increased her pace, as though by running faster she could leave all her problems behind. The waistband of her jeans gouged into her stomach with each movement of her legs. The stitch in her side evolved until she felt as though she might burst into flame or fall apart. Pulling in great gasping gulps of air, she dropped to her knees on the other side of the path and clutched handfuls of the spiky grass that grew there. She should walk after a long run, but her trembling legs could no longer support her.

How could she go back to maintaining a professional distance with Jonathan? If he suspected her motive in questioning the household and had initiated that kiss to detain or confuse her, then he had done a wham-bam job of it!

Had he discovered she was a private detective? Julie doubted it. If Jonathan had gotten wind of the fact that she was there to investigate him, she would have been fired and thrown out on her ear, she was sure. It would be better for everyone if Miss Vanderhoff found someone else. Except perhaps for Jon. The boy had grown close to Julie, and she hated to think what her leaving might do to him. Yet she wasn't qualified for this type of job! She did better behind the scenes and with the paperwork. She never should have agreed to this. She should have refused to see Miss Vanderhoff that day and closed up the office.

When her legs didn't feel so wobbly anymore, Julie stood and brushed the dirt from the seat of her jeans. A whirring engine caught her attention, the sound increasing in volume as a motorboat drew close. She looked over the cliff to see Sean MacPhearson take one hand off the wheel and wave.

Her first thought was to pretend she hadn't seen him and retrace her steps to the house. But it was obvious she had seen him. She gave a feeble wave in return.

He pointed to the path in front of her. "There's a cove up ahead—at the turn of the rocks!" he yelled. "Meet me there."

Before she could reply, he moved the throttle, and the motorboat sped away.

Frustrated, Julie looked behind her toward the house—a speck on the horizon—then ahead to where the path took a turn at the edge of a sharp drop-off. The maples hid whatever lay to the left. What could Sean want to talk with her about? She should walk away, contact Miss Vanderhoff, drop the case—but the inborn part of Julie that needed to know more, the curious side that had led her to become a detective, had her taking the path to the cove. She'd never gone this far.

The ground leveled out to a small, private beach. In the near distance a thick line of pine trees and tall grasses formed a backdrop to the light patch of sand. On both sides of the rocky inlet jagged cliffs spread out about a hundred feet from beach to sea, keeping the strip of sand protectively nestled at the bottom of the U-shaped area. Sean had already pulled his boat up to the short wooden pier. "How about a ride?"

Julie shielded the sun from her eyes with one hand and looked at the small, lightweight boat. "I sincerely doubt you go to sea in that."

He laughed. "You're right. It's a friend's. I promised him I'd take it out and check into a problem he's been having with the engine. It's good to go now, though."

"Where's your boat?"

"She's at the wharf in town. I have a fully rigged sloop with sleeping cabins and a galley."

Julie walked out onto the pier until she stood over Sean. "So tell me—do you come to this area of the coast often? I'd heard this land was privately owned."

"By your employer, of course." Sean gave a disgusted smirk. "But what he doesn't know won't hurt him."

His remark didn't make Julie think very highly of Sean. "You know Mr. Taylor?"

"Just what I've heard—and read. I've never met the man, though, and don't care to. Are you coming for a ride or not?"

Julie hesitated. The muscles in her legs ached from her run. She hadn't completely bounced back from her cold yet and still tired easily. "Can you take me to the house? I should return before Jon wakes up from his nap."

Sean nodded. "I know of a pier not far from there. I can drop you off at it." He held out a large hand to help her into the boat. She took the seat beside his, and he started the engine.

The cold, salty wind blew harder as the boat picked up speed, playing havoc with her curls. It had a freeing effect for Julie, and for a time she forgot everything and closed her eyes, reveling as the moist air rushed over her face, stealing her breath yet refreshing her. All too soon Julie felt the boat slow and heard the motor idle. She opened her eyes to see they'd arrived at a pier in a small inlet that wasn't as secluded as the last one. Trees grew to the water's edge. To the right rose a grassy hill leading to the house.

"Thanks for the ride." Julie moved to get out.

Sean put a hand to her forearm. "Would you like to go out sometime? I'd love to show you my *Bonny Lass*."

"Bonny Lass?"

"My boat."

"Oh. No, I don't think so, Sean, but thanks for asking."

"Well, if you change your mind, I plan to be in town for

awhile." Sean released her arm, and she offered him a faint smile before she stepped up onto the pier. "Good-bye, wee Sea Nymph," he teased.

Embarrassed, Julie strode up the hill. When she was within sight of the house, she thought she saw a face peering from one of the upstairs windows facing the pier, but at this distance it was too hard to tell.

"Just my imagination," she told herself under her breath when she came closer to the house and saw no one there. Julie opened the door and stepped inside the foyer. A shiver of apprehension tingled down her spine, convincing her something was amiss. She closed the door, and its soft click seemed to resound throughout the room. "I'm being ridiculous," she mumbled. "If I don't snap out of it, I'll wind up a basket case."

Humming to herself to break the pervasive quiet, Julie squared her shoulders, grabbed the banister and hurried upstairs to her room. As soon as she opened the door, she stopped, then froze in place, her eyes widening in alarm.

seven

The distinctive smell of watermelon bubble gum lingered in the air. Standing in the entrance to her room, Julie stared fixedly at the tall mirror above the pine dresser. Red block letters in a childish hand screamed at Julie from the silver glass.

Go away!!!! Nobodie wants you here!!!! If you stay here —you'll be merdered like she was!!!!

Julie frowned at the hate-filled message and clutched the doorframe with a shaky hand. Emily? It had to be. Then she believed her father to be a murderer—or perhaps she meant someone else? Whatever the case, the child obviously knew something she wasn't telling.

Julie moved to the bureau and picked up her open silver tube of Firelight Red lipstick, now smashed and ruined beyond repair. Tossing it into the trash container, she then plucked several tissues from a nearby box and attempted to wipe away the mess. The words smeared into one wavy, red splotch.

Just then she heard a splintering crash and a yelp from downstairs. She could feel her heart pounding in her throat, and the eyes staring back at her in the graffiti-stained mirror widened. She shut them briefly to gather her wits about her. Likely a maid had broken a dish or something. Still, she should investigate.

Crumpling the tissue in one hand, Julie left her room and went downstairs, her steps muffled by the carpet. Reaching the bottom of the staircase, she walked down the parquet floor of the silent hall. Light shone from a partially open door, in a room Julie had never visited. Pushing the door a few inches, she peeked inside.

Emily stood staring open-mouthed at a large portrait on the wall. A broken vase containing several stalks of lily-of-the-valley lay next to the child's feet, and water spread over the hardwood floor. Slim tapered candles had been lit and placed in stubby silver candleholders on a mahogany table underneath the portrait, reminding Julie of a shrine.

The little girl was unharmed, though obviously in a state of shock, and Julie looked up at the painting that so thoroughly captured her attention. It easily could have been a portrait of the child in twenty years—though Julie hoped not. The painting would have fit in well inside a French bistro. Taking a few steps into the room, Julie stared.

The young woman, whose alluring green eyes sparkled with mischief, daring, and fun, laughed down at them from the oil canvas. Sunny blond hair spilled from the fingers of one hand placed at the crown of her head, holding the thick tresses up off her neck in a seductive pose. Twin dimples winked from the corners of her full rosy lips in an angelic face that was deceiving—the woman's character clearly revealed by the sea-green negligee she wore, with one spaghetti strap hanging suggestively off her shoulder. Her other pink-tipped hand clutched her hip, which was thrust sideways. A drawstring at the ruffled neck lay open, shamelessly exposing an expanse of snowy white cleavage, and the filmy material of the gown revealed a shadowy outline of a small waist, curvy hips, and long legs beneath, leaving little to the imagination. Emily's mother?

A harsh gasp followed by a muttered expletive alerted Julie, and she turned and watched Jonathan march into the room. His stormy gaze sliced through her. "Who gave you permission to—?" He broke off as he caught sight of Emily staring trance-like, and his gaze followed his daughter's, lifting to the painting.

"Angela," he breathed, confirming Julie's suspicion that this was, indeed, the deceased Mrs. Taylor. Julie watched as shock, desire, hurt, and bitterness flitted through his eyes in rapid succession, and she turned her head away, uneasy.

"Emily Jewel Taylor!" he ground out in a low voice. "You know this room is off limits!"

For the first time the girl seemed to realize she wasn't alone. Turning, she blinked as if awakening from a deep sleep. Disillusionment and shock were written in her eyes. Obviously she had never seen this side of her mother.

"Daddy," she breathed. "I—I saw the glow and came to see what it was."

Jonathan's mouth narrowed, and he gave a curt nod. "Go to your room. We'll talk later."

The trembling child didn't hesitate. She escaped the room, carefully dodging her father who stood just inside the door. He turned his gaze to Julie. "And what is your excuse?"

"I heard a crash and came to investigate. The flowers!" she exclaimed, suddenly remembering the broken vase. Julie rushed over, hoping the water hadn't ruined the varnished wood floor, and looked around for something to sop up the spill.

"Leave it!" Jonathan ordered. "I have maids to take care of that sort of thing—speaking of which, where are they?" He stomped over to a built-in intercom on the wall. Punching a button he barked orders into the speaker and held a curt conversation with whomever was on the other side.

While he was thus occupied, Julie took her first good look at the room, evidently a parlor or den. A thick layer of dust shrouded the few pieces of carved mahogany furniture. The faded maroon-colored drape was shut tight against the daylight and a matching velvet sofa and two chairs sat waiting, obviously unused for some time. On the far side of the room a small alcove held a loveseat. The whole room appeared to have been neglected and forgotten.

Shannon hurried inside bearing a towel, broom, and dustpan. She stopped short when she caught sight of the portrait, and her mouth dropped open.

"Where's Mrs. Leighton?" Jonathan asked, his voice dangerously soft as he approached. "I distinctly remember telling her to come."

The girl shrugged. "I don't know, Mr. Taylor. She told me she had an important errand to take care of and that I was to come and clean up a broken vase."

"It figures." Jonathan pushed a shaky hand through his hair and closed his eyes briefly, apparently trying to calm down. "Very well. When she returns, tell her I wish to speak with her—immediately."

"Yes, sir," the maid replied. Averting her eyes from the come-hither painting, she made quick work of cleaning up the mess. Except for the sound of glass scraping across wood and onto metal, everything was starkly quiet.

As if invisible strings were pulling her head upward, Julie again looked at the painting. To say Angela Taylor had been outwardly beautiful would be a gross understatement. She had the allure of the fabled wanton siren that brought a man to imminent destruction at sea by wooing and trapping him from afar with her persuasive charms, never letting him suspect he was under her power. Totally enamored, the man would give himself over to her, and she would forever possess his soul, often destroying him in the process when his ship came too close and was dashed against the rocks.

Had Angela done something similar with Jonathan? Is that why he was often so distant? Was he forever snared by the memory of his wife's seducing beauty?

It was now laughable to Julie that she'd been concerned Jonathan might be starting to care for her. Angela had evidently been all a man could desire, and Julie was the complete opposite of the sensual woman.

"Miss Rae, meet Angela Taylor. My wife."

The words were mocking, curt. Julie turned her head his way. A hard expression veiled Jonathan's eyes as he stared at the painting.

"She was. . .beautiful," Julie managed, uncomfortable and unsure of what to say.

"Yes. Beautiful, desirable, spectacular—like a glittering diamond. And just as cold and hard and ruthless." At Julie's involuntary gasp, he looked at her. "The diamond is one of the hardest substances known to man, Miss Rae. Its many facets glimmer when light touches them, giving off spectacular color to dazzle the mind. But it can also cut almost anything without damage to itself. The only thing to cut a diamond is another diamond—equally cold and hard."

Julie contemplated his strange words. As she watched, he walked over to the low table, seeming to notice the lit candles for the first time. "What the—what is going on in this place?" His shocked voice dwindled away.

Reaching out, he snuffed the yellow flames with his fingertips. The maid hurried from the room, but Julie didn't move. She must gather what information she could—no matter how tasteless her job had suddenly become.

Jonathan plucked a discarded bundled sheet off the floor and tossed it to the sofa. Obviously the sheet had been used to cover the painting. He stood beneath the huge oil canvas and looked up at the colorful image of his wife.

"Angela gave that to me a year after Emily was born," he said, half to himself. "I thought it had been destroyed." He lifted a hand and touched the slim, green-clad body in the painting, letting his fingertips trail down the willowy form.

" 'The corrections of discipline are the way to life,' " he whispered, " 'keeping you from the immoral woman, from the smooth tongue of the wayward wife. Do not lust in your heart after her beauty or let her captivate you with her eyes, for the prostitute reduces you to a loaf of bread, and the adulteress preys upon your very life.' " As he spoke, his trembling hand slowly lowered until it hung at his side.

Julie's eyes widened in astonishment to hear verses from Proverbs come from his mouth. He glanced her way.

"Surprised?" He gave a dry, humorless laugh. "I came across that not long before her death." His gaze returned to the painting, and his body tensed as he continued to stare at it. "And I gave orders for *this* to be destroyed a long time ago."

With a muffled exclamation Jonathan suddenly wrenched

the massive portrait from the wall and slammed it onto the hardwood floor. The picture landed with a deafening crash, the sound reverberating throughout the room. Uneasy silence followed.

His tortured gaze lifted and met Julie's astonished one. He appeared shocked, as if he'd momentarily forgotten her presence; then the shuttered look returned to his eyes as his mask again slipped into place. He straightened to his full height.

"Tell the maid we have new fuel for the fireplace. Burn it," he ordered. "It should have been destroyed long ago." Pivoting on his heel, he left the room.

Julie's knees threatened to buckle, and she took the few steps to the sofa, carefully avoiding the broken frame of the canvas. Staring ahead at nothing, she sank to the faded cushion. A cloud of dust rose up and tickled her nose, making her sneeze. Julie dropped her head into her hands.

"Oh, dear God—help him," she whispered. "Help all of us. I don't know what's going on here anymore. An hour ago I was positive Jonathan didn't kill his wife, but after what I just saw—I don't know—"

Remembering the agony swimming in his gaze, Julie felt as though his pain were her own, as though it were her heart that was bleeding. No matter how she desired to ease his suffering, her presence would likely only inflict greater pain. Yet she must stay until her work was finished. Until the truth was exposed—no matter what it uncovered. A verse from First Corinthians floated through her mind: "Therefore judge nothing before the appointed time; wait till the Lord comes. He will bring to light what is hidden in darkness and will expose the motives of men's hearts."

"Dear Lord," Julie murmured into the empty room, "come and visit this house. And when the secrets hidden here are at last revealed—" She choked and for a moment couldn't continue. "Please, Lord, please—don't let it destroy the innocents."

❧

After seeking out the maid and relaying Jonathan's orders to have the demolished painting disposed of, Julie went up-stairs. Pausing in front of Jon's door, she opened it a crack and peeked inside.

A teddy bear nightlight shone in the darkened room, softly illuminating the round face on the pillow. One dimpled hand lay under his rosy cheek. His face in repose looked so inno-cent and sweet. Something stirred within Julie's breast and put a lump in her throat. She closed the door with a quiet click then moved to Emily's door. Hushed sobbing could be heard from within.

Julie hesitated. Would her company be welcomed or resented? She gave the door a gentle tap. The sobbing instantly stopped, and silence filled its place. Sighing, Julie had just turned away when she heard a feeble "Come in?"

Once inside, Julie looked at Emily and felt a stab of pity. Smudges of Firelight Red covered her cheeks from rubbing watery eyes with lipstick-smeared hands. Julie closed the door and approached the girl. "Are you okay, Emily?"

Dislike, distrust, and fear broadcast themselves silently to Julie from the child's eyes. The girl nodded with clenched lips.

Julie dropped in the wicker wastebasket the crumpled tissue she'd been holding since leaving her room. She plucked a few more tissues from the box on the night table and, to Emily's obvious surprise, gently began cleaning the defiant face.

"Firelight Red isn't easy to get off," Julie murmured. "We may have to use soap and water."

The girl jerked her head back, startled. A fleeting expres-sion of guilt clouded her eyes, followed by anger. She moved backward over her mattress, away from Julie's tender minis-trations. "I don't need you! Why don't you go back to wher-ever you're from and leave us alone?"

"I'm sorry you feel that way, Emily. I was hoping we could be friends."

The child stared down at her ruffled pink bedspread. "I don't like you. And my daddy doesn't either!" Her gaze shot up, her lips forming a cruel little smile. "My mommy was lots prettier than you!"

Julie felt a twinge at the barbed words designed to wound. Yet she recognized them for what they were—the defenses of an emotionally disturbed little girl desperately trying to order her small world and make it right again.

"Yes, your mother was very beautiful. And I know you must have loved her a great deal. But I'm not trying to take her place. I want you to know that. And I want to be your friend."

The little chin sailed up. "I don't need any friends."

Julie smiled. "Oh, yes, you do. Everyone needs someone to talk to when they're hurting. To share good times with— and bad ones."

Emily paused, seeming to consider. "I had a friend once. She was my best friend in the whole world. But Daddy won't let me play with her anymore." She looked away.

Julie heard pain lace the wistful voice. What was wrong with that man? Didn't he realize what he was doing to his children by forcing them to live such a cloistered life?

"I have a best friend too," Julie said. "Jesus is my best friend, and He's always there when I need Him. Even when I'm alone, He's with me."

Emily tilted her head curiously. "How can somebody be your friend if you can't see them?"

"Jesus can. Whenever I feel sad or scared, I pray to Jesus, and He makes me feel better. He can help you too."

Emily was silent a long time then looked down at her balled, red-stained hands. "I'm sorry I ruined your lipstick."

"I understand, and I forgive you." Julie held a hand out to her, hoping for a hug.

The girl shrank back against the pillow. "But I still don't want to be your friend," she stated firmly. Her eyes flashed at Julie and issued a warning: Stay away.

Julie sighed. Emily was so like her father it wasn't funny.

Withdrawing her hand, Julie let it settle back onto her lap. "That's okay, Emily. You don't have to be my friend. But I'll always be yours."

The child didn't respond, only stared at the opposite wall, frowning. Deciding it was time to go, Julie rose from the bed.

୬

The next morning Julie combed her hair for the third time, painted her nails with a shimmery silver polish, fiddled with the collar of her rayon blouse—anything to avoid going downstairs and facing Jonathan. He usually left the table after he finished breakfast, leaving the others still eating. If she timed it right, Julie would miss him. She had awakened with a headache and asked Shannon to see to getting the children to breakfast. Aspirin had alleviated the pain thirty minutes later, but she remained in her room.

Her stomach growled, reminding her she'd barely touched dinner last night. She grabbed a tumbler of water from the bedside table and gulped it down. Unfortunately it didn't do much to relieve the gnawing hunger pangs. Her gaze wandered to her purse. Last time she looked she'd had a box of breath mints inside. How many of those could a person eat without getting a sugar rush?

A knock on the door was followed by Shannon's appearance. "Sorry to bother you, but Mr. Taylor would like to speak with you in the library if you're feeling up to it."

Julie's fingers tightened around the plastic glass she still held, and she set it down carefully. "Thank you. Please tell him I'll be there shortly."

The maid gave her a peculiar look but said nothing more and left. Julie studied her reflection in the mirror, striving to compose herself. *What's wrong with me? I'm hardly acting like a professional detective—more like a nervous schoolgirl about to be reprimanded by the principal.*

But she wasn't the one who had done anything wrong.

Jonathan's behavior the previous afternoon embarrassed, dismayed and, yes—even frightened her. Exactly who was Jonathan Taylor? Absent father? Grieved husband? Guilt-ridden murderer? Something deep within Julie pleaded his case, whispering his innocence.

Exiting her room, she blanked out her thoughts, attempting to achieve a more professional frame of mind before meeting with Jonathan. At the double doors leading to the library, Julie halted, then knocked, waiting for his summons.

Upon entering the room she noticed the barely discernible shadows that lay under his eyes, as well as in them. Still, Jonathan managed to overpower the room with his commanding presence.

"Are you well?" he asked. "We missed you at breakfast. I hope you're not sick again."

"No, I'm fine." Julie tried to make her voice sound casual.

He studied her as though he didn't believe her.

"Really, I'm okay," Julie said.

He nodded. "Sit down," he said quietly before turning to look out the window facing the garden.

Julie slid onto the leather-upholstered chair and clasped her hands around her crossed knees to prevent them from shaking.

"It has come to my attention that you've taken the children to church services in town."

Julie nodded then realized he couldn't see her. "Yes, I did."

"You're not to do so again."

She blinked. "But why? I think it's important for them to receive a Christian education. Don't you. . . ?" She trailed off weakly when he faced her, his features hardened.

"No, I don't. Through personal experience I've found that some claim to be members of the Christian faith but are nothing more than a bunch of hypocrites—hiding something that, if found out, would be detrimental to their good name." His hands went to the top of the opposite chair, and he leaned toward her. "You're not to go there again."

"Now just one minute." A fire kindled inside Julie, dispelling her nervousness. "It's one thing for you to tell me not to take your children to church. But it's quite another for you to order me not to go!"

She sat up straighter. "You have no right to interfere in my personal life. No matter how you feel about Christianity, it doesn't give you an excuse to order me around as if I were a puppet pulled by your strings."

He frowned. "I don't want my children going to that church."

"Then I'll find someone to watch them for a few hours while I go. I won't be denied the opportunity to worship with other believers. And if you refuse me, then I'll have no alternative but to hand in my notice."

Quiet permeated the room after her impromptu ultimatum.

Julie's fingers dug into the armrests when she realized what she had done. She had given him an opportunity to fire her. She had jeopardized the investigation as effectively as shackling handcuffs to her wrists and tossing him the key.

Jonathan moved to the front of his chair, sat down, and leaned toward her. "Would you really do that, Miss Rae?" he asked in a low voice, a challenging light in his eyes. "Would you give up your job for your faith?"

Julie hesitated then lifted her chin and gave a tight nod. No one would come between her and her Lord. Besides, losing this job didn't mean she couldn't continue working on the case. It might be harder to gather information, but she could do it.

He studied her for what seemed eons to Julie. She swallowed hard but refused to look away, giving him back stare for stare.

Slowly he nodded. "All right. If you can find someone to take care of the children while you go to that church," he said as though the words left a bitter taste in his mouth, "then I won't stop you. But remember—the children come first."

I could say the same to you, Julie thought but didn't speak it. "Thank you, Mr. Taylor."

He rose and headed back toward the window, putting a hand inside his pants pocket. The jingling of change was a sign to Julie of his unusual nervousness.

"One more thing. About yesterday—" he started then hesitated. A few seconds elapsed before he continued. "I shouldn't have said what I did, even if it is true. That door is always kept locked—the room is no longer used—and seeing the picture again caught me off guard." He turned to face her, his eyes almost pleading with her to understand. "I gave orders to have the painting thrown out after Angela's death. Seeing it—in that room—brought back bad memories—though some are impossible to escape and have become my daily companions. I've tried to let go, but it's no use. . . ."

Julie barely nodded, uncertain how to respond. The room must have been where he and Angela last fought. Yet he didn't know she was a private investigator, so why was he opening up to her, sharing a confidence—as he had on the beach yesterday? Perhaps that was why. She was evidently the only one who believed him. And that must be what had prompted him to kiss her. Gratitude. Nothing more.

Jonathan stared at her a moment longer before turning back to the window. "That will be all. You may go now."

Relieved, Julie went to the door, opened it, and paused. It struck her that she should discuss what had happened with Emily yesterday. Turning, she opened her mouth to speak, but the words never left her.

Jonathan's head was bowed, as though in defeat. Suddenly he didn't look so powerful. Every instinct in Julie propelled her to go to him, but instead she resisted, backed out of the room, and closed the door.

Her emotions had become hopelessly entangled and confused where Jonathan was concerned. Even if he wasn't a suspected murderer, even if he didn't prefer voluptuous blondes to short brunettes, and the relationship between her and Jonathan could be considered normal—there could be no relationship. He didn't serve her Lord. In fact, in light of their recent conversation Julie felt it safe to say Jonathan wanted nothing to do with God.

It would be paramount to speed up the investigation, if possible, finish her job, and leave this place. And Julie determined to do just that.

eight

The next morning Jonathan left on business for a few days. Julie wouldn't have even known he was gone if she hadn't overheard a conversation between the hired help. Jonathan had avoided her since their talk in the library. Though relieved, Julie also felt depressed by his absence and upbraided her reflection severely.

"I'm glad he's gone. It will make the investigation easier. I won't have to worry about suddenly running into him every minute of the day."

Sad brown eyes stared back, reminding her he hadn't even said good-bye. Tempted to throw the comb she held at the woebegone image in the mirror, Julie made a point of setting it carefully on the dresser instead. Her gaze went to a small picture of her and her father taken several years ago in front of their summer beachfront cottage. She picked up the frame. His pale blue eyes, shrewd yet gentle, smiled at her from the picture. Julie traced her index finger over his image then sighed and placed it back on the dresser.

What would her father say concerning her unprofessional behavior? In past cases she'd always been able to maintain a civil yet distant relationship with those with whom she came in contact. The present case was the exception to the rule. Of course, undercover work was new to her and quite obviously not her niche. Since she had come to the Taylor residence, nothing seemed to work right. Her intelligent brain, her con-tained emotions, her cool demeanor—all seemed to have been left behind in Locklin.

She drew in a lung full of air and exhaled it harshly. With a few quick jerks she tied the green silk tie at the neckline of her blouse. What had happened to self-assured, competent

Julie Daniels, private investigator?

A timid knock interrupted her disgusted perusal, and she walked to the door and opened it. Jon stood there, tears glazing his eyes. "I want to go with you," he sobbed.

Julie crouched beside him and brushed his wet cheeks with her fingertips. "Not this time, Honey."

"We went with you last time."

His voice was insistent, grating on Julie's already worn nerves. She hadn't told Emily and Jon that Jonathan had forbidden their attendance at church. She didn't want to build any more walls between them and their father. There were enough already.

"Tell you what," Julie said, forcing a smile. "When I get back, how about if you and I and Emily go for a picnic?"

He sniffled. "Promise you'll come back?"

The pitiful words pierced Julie, and she drew him close. Almost everyone he knew had left him in some way. His mother—by her death. His father—by distancing himself from the boy. His relatives—by his father's forced isolation of the children.

"Of course I will," she murmured. "You can depend on it. And when I come back, we'll have a great time. You might even ask Mrs. Leighton to fix some of those sardine sandwiches with that sandwich spread you like."

Excitement lit his eyes. "The cook made chocolate cake last night," he exclaimed. "Can we have that too?"

Julie laughed and rumpled his dark hair. "Sure. I love Mrs. Ruggles's chocolate cake."

"I'll go ask right now!"

As she watched the boy run from the room, her heart ached for him. Both Taylor children owned what must be hundreds of toys and games but were lonely for companionship. They needed friends their own age with whom to play. It wasn't right or fair of Jonathan to deny them that privilege. But how could Julie broach the subject to their unapproachable father and make him understand? She had tried, but he had turned a deaf ear each time.

An hour later, while she sat in church and listened to the assistant pastor preach, Julie focused on the message: "Lean not on your own understanding; in all your ways acknowledge him, and he will make your paths straight."

Julie pondered the words. How much of her investigation had she turned over to God? Not all of it—that was for sure. Too busy trying to figure everything out on her own steam, she'd never taken the time to commit the entire case to Him— just bits and pieces here and there. No wonder she was floundering and hadn't gained any new ground! Closing her eyes, Julie released everything, including the unwanted feelings she had for the children's father, to her heavenly Counselor.

Immediately she received an answer in the depths of her spirit. *Stay after the service.*

Her logic deliberated. Why should she hang around an empty building? She couldn't query Pastor MacPhearson about the case since the assistant pastor mentioned he was out of town, acting as visiting preacher at another church. Besides, wouldn't everyone be leaving to go home?

Lean not unto your own understanding.

Julie furrowed her brow, puzzled, but confident the Good Shepherd was leading her.

The dismissal was given, and the people flocked to the back. Pastor MacPhearson's wife caught sight of Julie. "Miss Rae," she said happily as she bustled up to her. "I'm delighted you've come. But where are the children?"

"I wasn't able to bring them today."

"Oh, that's too bad. You'll stay for the meal, though, won't you?"

"Meal?"

The woman nodded. "Our fellowship potluck dinner. It was supposed to take place later in the month, but we had to move it to this week instead."

You know all, Lord.

Julie's smile faded. "Perhaps I should run to the store and

pick up some chips or a macaroni salad or something?"

"Oh, no—don't worry about it. There's plenty of food," Mrs. MacPhearson assured her. "We eat in the fellowship hall next door. I'll take you there."

Ten minutes later, Julie grabbed her heaping plate filled with more goodies than she knew she would ever eat. Mrs. MacPhearson had been insistent, even spooning helpings of casseroles and vegetables onto Julie's plate, like a mother would do for her child, and clucking her tongue and saying Julie was too thin. Julie wasn't offended; she knew the grandmotherly woman spoke only out of concern. The investigation had been a strain, both physically and mentally, and had affected Julie's appetite, as had the previous month of grieving for her father.

Mrs. MacPhearson found a spot for Julie at one of the nearby cafeteria-type tables. After making introductions between Julie and the young woman who sat on the other side, she hurried away to tend to something else.

The girl, who'd been introduced as Ginny, lifted a forkful of coleslaw to her mouth, studying Julie the entire time. "You work for Jonathan Taylor, don't you?"

Julie set down her cup of tea and regarded the woman with surprise. "Yes. How did you know?"

Ginny shrugged. "Word gets around in a town this size." She took another bite of food. "How is Jonathan? We really miss him."

"Miss him?" Julie parroted.

Ginny nodded. "My daughter Beth—the one over there with the French braid?" She pointed to a little blond girl about Emily's age who stood at the dessert table, giving its contents careful consideration. "She really likes Jonathan. He's good with kids. He sort of took the place of Beth's father." Ginny looked down at her plate, biting her lip. "My husband and I divorced when Beth was only a baby, and he hasn't come around to see her."

Julie blinked in amazement. Jonathan Taylor—good with

kids? Were they talking about the same man?

Ginny took a bite of smoked mackerel, her expression thoughtful. "Beth misses Emily too. They were best friends. But then Jonathan took Emily out of school after his wife died and hired a private tutor for her and Jon. Of course, I know it was hard for everyone involved—but that was a lot of claptrap Bessie Lou dished out about him murdering his wife. Jonathan Taylor wouldn't harm a gnat!" Golden brown eyes blazing, she set her fork down hard. "He's the kindest, dearest, sweetest man I've ever met."

And you're in love with him, Julie added silently, seeing more than anger blaze from the eyes of the pretty young woman. Something akin to jealousy stabbed Julie, surprising her. She averted her gaze.

"I think it's terrible how certain members of his staff turned on him!" Ginny exclaimed. "Bessie Lou is nothing more than a Southern hussy who loves to gossip. I doubt she heard any of the conversation between Jonathan and his wife that night."

Julie lifted a brow. "Why do you say that?"

Ginny shrugged, seeming to realize how adamant she'd become. Several at the table were giving her curious glances. She made an obvious effort to calm down as she took a long swallow of her drink. "Oh, nothing—just a hunch. Every time she tells the story, she gives it another twist."

Ginny sighed. "After Mrs. Taylor's death, Jonathan stopped coming to church. It's so sad—he was so on fire for the Lord, like most new Christians are."

Julie almost choked on the three-bean salad she was swallowing. Jonathan Taylor went to church and was on fire for the Lord? And he was a Christian? The same Jonathan Taylor who'd explicitly forbidden his children to attend worship services and had mocked everything Julie held sacred?

Julie knew she must look like a fish and made a conscious effort to close her gaping mouth while her mind tried to assimilate this new set of startling facts.

Beth skipped over to the table, a raisin cookie in one hand, a frosted cupcake in the other, and asked if she could play on the swing set. Ginny replied by pointing to the child's full dinner plate. Reluctantly the girl slid onto her chair, set her treats down, picked up her fork, and began to twirl her spaghetti.

"Beth, this is Miss Rae. She works for the Taylors."

A wistful expression lit Beth's pale blue eyes. "Is Jonathan coming again someday? And will he bring Emily too?"

"I hope so, Beth," Julie said. Well, Jonathan certainly had made a hit with this family. But why couldn't he get along with his own children? What caused such a drastic change? The death of his wife and the people's view that he'd been the cause of it? True, that would make anyone bitter, but Julie sensed more was involved and that the answer was more complex than a simple explanation could give.

As she tried to finish what was on her plate, Julie silently repeated her prayer that God would use her as His beacon of truth to scatter the darkness.

❧

When Julie returned to the Taylor residence, Jon almost knocked her down in his excitement.

"Are we going on the picnic now—huh, Julie?"

Emily stood a few feet away, a bored expression on her face, a wooden hamper over one arm. Julie noted the resigned look in the girl's cold green eyes and gave an inward sigh. Would she ever break through the barrier Emily had erected?

After promising an impatient Jon she would return in less than five minutes, Julie hurried upstairs to her room and changed into a purple T-shirt, a pair of comfortable jeans, and sneakers. She grabbed her windbreaker and hurried back downstairs.

Jon jumped up from the bottom step and grabbed her hand impatiently. "Come on," he insisted while tugging her arm. "You took forever."

Laughing, Julie allowed him to pull her outside. A solemn Emily trailed behind with the picnic basket.

The day was windy, though not cold. A pale sun floated amid gray-tinged clouds that sailed past a dusky-blue sky. The sea air was invigorating, as was the sound of the surf rushing at the rocks and landing with a thunderous crash. They walked the distance to the hidden cove, and Julie smiled upon reaching it, claiming it perfect for their picnic.

Jon and Emily scanned the wet sand for shells and other half-buried treasures the sea might have coughed up. Julie kicked off her tennis shoes and scrunched her toes into the damp earth, enjoying both the feel of it and the way the sand shifted beneath her feet when the icy water hit her ankles then receded. Smiling, she watched Emily and Jon play a game of tag with the ocean, the ocean winning every time.

A desire sparked to life inside Julie like a match suddenly struck. For the first time in her life, career wasn't enough for her. She wanted a husband. . .children.

The need was so intense that Julie abruptly turned away from the sight of Emily and Jon frolicking like young pups. Instead she concentrated on preparing for their picnic. When all was ready, she called the children, and they left their play to skip over and plunk themselves down on the blanket she had laid out. Invigorated and rosy with exercise, Emily had shed her solemn expression and even smiled when Julie handed her a sandwich. Julie's spirits lifted, and she smiled back.

An unusual lunch of Taylor brand sardines smothered in mayonnaise and mustard, with relish, sliced cucumbers, red onions, and tomatoes, followed. Jon proudly announced the contents were his idea and that Mrs. Leighton had given him free rein in the kitchen. Julie made a mental note to talk to the housekeeper.

"Let's make a sandcastle!" Jon exclaimed, his sandwich eaten. "A pirate castle!"

"Sounds like an idea," Julie agreed, wrapping up the rest of her sandwich.

"Pirates don't have castles, Dummy," Emily argued.

"Emily—" Julie said in warning.

Jon lifted his chin with an air of superiority. "Well, mine do! They have to go somewhere when they get off their ships. And since they have lots of gold and jewels and stuff, they can buy a castle with their loot."

Emily rolled her eyes, and Julie grinned.

The wind had picked up some, but the children didn't seem to mind. As Julie cupped her hand around the sand, trying to form a sad excuse for a round turret, she was grateful for the breakthrough. They were laughing and playing together in unity—a first since her arrival weeks ago.

So involved were the trio in building walls, turrets, and a moat that they didn't notice the first splatters of rain. Suddenly the sky opened, demanding their attention and drenching them within seconds. Julie looked up in surprise, blinking as pellets of icy water blinded her. When had the sky grown so dark?

Hurrying to gather their things into the picnic basket, she scanned the surroundings for temporary cover. It was over a mile back to the house; they would be soaked by the time they got there. Correction—they already were. Julie moaned inwardly. Once again she'd blown it.

She heard a faint sound, barely discernible above the rain pounding on sand and rocks and the children's squeals. A boat approached the pier, slapping the turbulent dark green waves and once coming dangerously close to the rocks. A man stood behind the wheel, motioning them over. He, too, was soaked to the skin, and it was a moment before Julie recognized Sean underneath the wet-darkened hair.

She abandoned the basket and grabbed Jon's and Emily's hands. The trio moved up the narrow pier slick from the rain. Every third or fourth board was bowed from weathering. The wide cracks between each of the planks didn't do much for Julie's peace of mind—especially with the rain beating down on her and the children, further slowing their progress.

Sean quickly hoisted first Jon, then Emily over the side. Next he reached for Julie, lifted her, and swung her over, setting her on the deck beside him.

"Get below!" he yelled over a roll of thunder. "Weather's too dangerous to try to make it out of here. We'll have to wait 'til this blows over. I don't want to risk the possibility of getting smashed against the rocks a second time."

Julie shivered, glancing at the cliffs that rose up on both sides of the inlet. She'd never really noticed how close the unforgiving rocks were to the pier.

"Can I help? I know how to tie the right kinds of knots. I used to sail some."

Relief covered his wet features. "Secure those lines." He nodded toward the stern. "I'll take care of the rest."

Julie ordered the children to take shelter below then hurried to do as he'd said.

❧

Minutes later, behind the privacy of the closed bathroom door, Julie helped divest the children of their sodden clothing and rubbed them dry with towels before doing the same for herself. The T-shirts Sean had loaned them until their own clothes were dry came to Jon's ankles, Emily's calves, and just above Julie's knees. Julie laughed, hoping to dispel the children's gloom.

"Don't we look a sight!" she exclaimed with a smile.

Emily merely looked at her and flicked wet strands of long hair from her face, tucking them behind her ears.

"Awww. I look like a girl," Jon said, disgusted.

Julie ruffled his hair and smiled. "It's only for awhile. Just until our clothes are dry. Besides, pirates used to wear overly long shirts, I think."

"Really?" That seemed to mollify the boy.

For good measure Julie wrapped and tucked one of the dry towels around her hips for modesty's sake. She then opened the accordion door, and they left the cramped quarters to join Sean in the salon.

Teak and brass were predominant, and though the cabin wasn't large, it was cleverly designed to use every available space. Two long, cushioned seats were built into opposite sides of the wall, and built in cabinets and drawers filled the area.

"Nice boat," Julie said.

Sean had changed to dry clothes and sat on one of the cushions. "It's not as big or as nice as the one I had before, but it suits my purposes."

Julie fingered her damp hair.

"Need a blow dryer?" Sean offered. "I have one—somewhere. I don't use it much."

"No, thanks. My hair dries fast since it's short. But maybe Emily should use it. Her hair is long, and I wouldn't want her to catch cold—"

"I don't want to use anything of his," Emily stated, an icy look in her eyes. "And I wish I didn't have to wear his crummy old shirt or be on his stupid boat either."

"Emily!" Julie exclaimed, shocked. "Mr. MacPhearson has been a big help to us. If he hadn't come along, we'd still be out there in the storm. You're not being very nice."

Emily shrugged and looked away. "I don't care. I'd rather be dead than be here with him."

Julie knew she should again reprimand Emily and make her apologize, but seeing the stubborn tilt of her chin, Julie surmised such an order would prove useless. Again Julie saw traces of Jonathan in the child.

"It's okay," Sean said with a faint smile. "Don't push the wee lass. I'm sure she didn't mean it—"

"Yes, I did!" Emily shot back, her words coming fast and furious. "I meant all of it! I don't like you, and I don't like you"—this directed to Julie—"and I wish you'd all leave me alone and go away!" She ran back to the bathroom and slammed the door behind her, leaving an uneasy quiet in the main cabin, broken only by the rain thrumming against the boat.

Feeling unsteady, both from the rocking vessel and Emily's behavior, Julie sank onto the seat opposite Sean. Jon took a place beside her. She tried to think of something to say after such an embarrassing scene, but nothing came to mind.

"Wow! Did you do that?" Jon asked.

Julie looked to the paneled wall where Jon pointed. A

framed watercolor painting of a glorious sunrise over the ocean, as seen from between palm fronds on an island beach, graced the wall.

"Aye, that I did," Sean said with a nod.

"I like to draw too," Jon confided, "but Emily never gives me paper. She said she doesn't want to tear any out of her drawing book and ruin it."

Julie wondered, with the quantity of toys and games that had been heaped upon the children, why no one had thought to buy Jon a sketchpad if that was his heart's desire.

Sean chuckled. "I might have a spare around here I could give you."

Jon's eyes brightened. "Really? Wow. But I could never draw as good as you." His gaze went back to the picture. "My mommy used to draw too. Only she drew apples and stuff."

Sean was quiet a moment, and when he spoke again his voice was soft. "What you're looking at, Jon, is an island on the Pacific—a lovely spot full of mystery and romance." When Sean said the last, he looked at Julie, and she squirmed, suddenly uncomfortable.

"What's miseree and romance?" Jon questioned.

Sean let out a great laugh. "You have that right, me boy! The two go together, hand in hand. Romance often leads to misery—don't you think so, Julie?"

She ignored his baited question and quietly addressed Jon. "Romance is what God intended between two people who love each other and want to marry or who are already married. And mystery is the wonder behind it all."

"Oh," Jon muttered, disappointed. "I thought mystery was like in spy stories and stuff."

"Well, yes, it can be that too," Julie said.

Jon's attention focused on a ship model sitting nearby, and his eyes lit up as he shot questions at Sean with the rapid-fire speed of a machine gun.

Julie listened to Sean's answers, noticing the way the man kept glancing in her direction. His eyes held puzzlement, curiosity, as if she were a rare species of fish he'd never come across.

Julie fidgeted and suddenly realized she still held their bundled wet clothes in a towel. She unrolled it, pulled Emily's striped shirt out and smoothed the wrinkles.

"Give me the clothes," Sean said, rising from his chair. "I'll put them next to the stove so they dry faster."

After Sean went down the narrow corridor to the galley, Jon turned to Julie. "Is he going to cook our clothes?" he asked, his eyes wide.

She shook her head no and smiled, holding her arms out to him. Jon gladly accepted the invitation, snuggling against her chest like a baby cub to its mother. Julie felt the stirrings of that same yearning she'd experienced an hour ago, to have a family of her own. She tightened her arms around the boy and dropped a light kiss on top of his damp head.

Jon looked up. "Will you stay with us forever and ever?"

His wistful question brought to mind her reason for being in Maine. She loosened her grip, mentally distancing herself from the boy. "Forever is a long time, Jon. I can't make a promise like that."

Jon's downcast face tore at Julie's heart. Despite her better judgment, she added, "I'll be here as long as you need me."

His eyes lit up. "I'll always need you, Miss Julie." He punctuated his declaration with a hug.

His words nagged at Julie for the next hour of their stay on the *Bonny Lass*. Sean brought steaming mugs of instant hot chocolate. Yet no matter how hard Julie tried to coax Emily into joining them, her words directed to the closed accordion door went unheeded.

Julie returned to see Sean and Jon on the floor in a serious game of Go-Fish. As she watched the two curly heads, one russet, the other raven-haired, intently bent over their hands, it came to Julie what a wonderful father Sean would make, should he ever put down roots long enough to marry. If only Jonathan would show the same kind of interest in his son.

Soon the staccato beats of pelting rain dwindled to a softer and slower plopping sound. Sean looked up from his place on the floor. "It's clearing. But I doubt your clothes are dry. You're welcome to stay."

"Please, Julie," Jon said. "And you play with us this time."

"Well, all right," Julie agreed. "But only one game."

Thirty minutes later, after she'd repeatedly given into Jon's pleas for "just one more game," Julie firmly announced they should go before Mrs. Leighton sent the Coast Guard out looking for them. Julie retrieved their slightly damp clothes and steered Jon back to the accordion door. Emily said nothing, sat on the closed toilet lid and received her clothes with a petulant frown, obviously still put out.

Soon, Sean guided his boat to the cove near the house and helped them step onto the wet pier. "Hope you're not in too much trouble," he said to Julie after she thanked him.

"Mr. Taylor is out of town," she said. "Still I'm sure he would have understood, given the circumstances."

Sean let out a snort. "I'd heard his character wasn't quite so obliging." He continued to stare at Julie, as though preoccupied about something, then shrugged and waved, pulling the *Bonny Lass* away from the pier.

"I'm glad we're off his dumb boat," Emily said, staring at the departing Sean, her features pulled into a grimace. "I wish he would have been the one to drown instead of Mommy. I hate him!"

"Emily!" Julie gasped in shock. Yet before she could say another word, the little girl turned and ran to the house.

⬥

That night, long after the household had gone to bed, Julie found an opportunity to slip from her room and downstairs to Jonathan's office. Once inside, she closed the door. With the aid of her pocket flashlight, she hurried across the room to his desk and switched on the small lamp there, turning its beam away from the room's entrance. She didn't want any light seeping under the door, alerting anyone to her presence.

She took a seat in the rolling chair, glancing at the desk drawers. She had tried them earlier when she'd first come to the Taylor residence and Jonathan had gone on that first business trip, but they had been locked. Curiously she tried the top one now. Still locked.

Flicking the switch on the desktop computer, she brought it to life, cringing when it made its customary humming and bleeping noises as it went through the usual warm-up process. She tapped into the Internet, but when she tried to get into her private E-mail account she found her server was down.

Letting out a frustrated breath, she studied the icons displayed on the desk top. Relief hit her when she saw that Jonathan had E-mail, and she moved the mouse to click on it. Grateful to discover he used the automatic password feature, she hurriedly composed a message to her secretary, informing her to contact Claire Vanderhoff with the update: "Investigation proceeding as planned. Nothing new uncovered. Will contact in another month." Then, to her secretary, Julie typed a message asking if Dale had uncovered anything about the case and directed her to send any information to the post office box Julie had recently acquired. She also gave her Bessie Lou's name, as well as Clancy's and the other employees of the Taylor residence, asking for a full bio on each of them.

Hearing a noise in the hall, Julie paused, her hands freezing over the keyboard. She snapped out of her shock and turned off the lamp. Barely breathing, she waited in the semi-darkness, the glow from the monitor casting a bluish tinge over her stricken face.

Had Jonathan returned from his business trip early? Would he walk in at any moment and catch Julie in the act? What excuse could she give for using his computer? True, she had asked to borrow it to search for a Christian book website the week she had arrived there, but she didn't think Jonathan would appreciate her being here without his permission, especially in the dead of night.

Hurriedly she moved the mouse to "send" and clicked the button, mildly relieved when she saw the tiny image of a letter fly from the box, indicating her message was being delivered. After "Success!" appeared on the screen, she called up the list of messages sent, located the one she had just typed, and hit the delete button, erasing all evidence of her message from the file folder.

She hit "shut down" then waited until the screen told her it was safe to turn off the computer. As she reached for the switch, she knocked over a canister of pens. A loud clatter broke the silence. All the pens went sailing to the carpet.

With her heart beating rapidly, Julie righted the canister, waiting for someone to come barging through the study door, demanding to know what she was doing there at half past midnight. When nothing happened, Julie exhaled with relief and bent to pick up the pens, afterward getting on her hands and knees to look under the desk and see if any had rolled underneath. One had.

As Julie reached for it, she noticed a small, crumpled paper ball underneath the massive desk, out of reach of a vacuum cleaner. Julie groped for the paper wad, her fingers barely touching it. She scanned the contents on the desktop and snatched up a ruler, using it to bat the paper out the other side. Rising, she moved to the front of the desk and plucked up the paper ball.

Carefully she unraveled and smoothed the dusty ivory rectangle—obviously under the desk a long time, hidden from any maid's view—and looked at a statement of a paid bill from a local detective agency. It was dated over a year and a half ago.

Her brows drew downward. So Jonathan had hired a private detective. For business reasons? Personal ones?

Realizing she'd been in Jonathan's office much too long, Julie tucked the paper in her sweatpants pocket, grabbed her slim flashlight, turned it on, and switched off the desk lamp. Letting herself out, she closed the door without making a sound and hurried into the corridor and toward the stairs. Tiny hairs prickled on the back of her neck, and she turned to look over her shoulder.

The room was pitch dark and appeared as empty as it had before, with only the obscure shadowy forms of furniture blending into the darkness. Still, Julie couldn't help but feel someone was watching. She sprinted up the carpeted steps, relieved when she arrived at her bedroom door. Shutting herself inside, she twisted the lock firmly.

nine

The fears of the night seemed groundless in the cheery light of morning. Almost ridiculous, really.

Julie and the children ate bacon, eggs, and cinnamon toast in the cozy breakfast room with its bay window looking out to the bright eastern skies. Below, the sea was somewhat calm, the wind leaving its signature of ripples over the silver water.

Emily and Jon headed for the playroom, and Julie located a local telephone directory to look in the business pages for Fielder Detective Agency. There was no listing. Next she checked the residential pages, but no Dan Fielder or D. Fielder was listed. Frustrated, she slammed the book shut and drummed her fingers on the table. *What now, Lord?*

She pursed her mouth thoughtfully then picked up the phone and dialed information, asking for the number of Fielder Detective Agency on Nantuckett Road. After a short wait, the aloof operator informed her there was no such listing. Julie replaced the receiver. Great. A dead end. Just when she thought she'd found a lead.

The instrument gave a shrill ring beneath her fingertips, startling her. Julie drew in a breath to calm her nerves and picked up the receiver. "Taylor residence."

"I'd like to speak to the bonny wee nanny who takes care of the Taylor children."

Despite her sour mood, Julie grinned. "Hi, Sean. What did you need?"

"I was calling to see if you'd like to go to dinner with me tonight."

"Tonight?" Julie asked.

"Aye. A local restaurant is running an all-you-can-eat special. They have great food. They're located on the coast, so they have a great view of the ocean too."

His wheedling made Julie roll her eyes. Well, why not? She needed a break from the house, and she could mix business and pleasure at the same time. She'd never really had an opportunity to question Sean.

"If Mrs. Leighton agrees to watch the kids, I'll go." Julie was ninety-nine per cent certain she would. The housekeeper doted on the children from what Julie had seen.

A pause. "What finally got you to say yes? My charming personality? My rugged good looks? Or was it simply the lure of good food in the best restaurant in town?"

Julie chuckled. "Maybe it had to do with your total lack of immodesty?"

"Ouch. That hurt," he said in amusement. "I'll pick you up at the pier near the house at seven. . . Julie?"

"Seven it is. See you then."

She replaced the receiver, staring at it. Sean was a nice guy, too much of a charmer for her liking, but someone she'd enjoy an evening with. So why did she suddenly feel leery of going with him? Because all she could think about was Jonathan and how he might construe the outing if he were here? Frustrated with herself, she left the table.

At six forty-five, she looked into the playroom. Jon was walking green plastic soldiers up the gangplank of a toy pirate ship while Emily sketched in her pad. Hearing the squeak of the door, the girl looked up, her gaze flying to Julie's. She snapped shut the cover of the pad and folded her arms over it in a protective gesture. Julie sighed.

"I'm leaving soon, but I'll be back later tonight to tuck you guys in," she said.

"You're going away?" Jon asked, on a plaintive note.

"Just for a few hours with Sean. You remember, the nice man who rescued us and took us on his boat when we got caught in the rain?" Jon nodded and gave a grudging smile, but Emily jumped up from her chair.

"You're going with him?" she cried, her expression full of

hatred. "Then I hope you never come back! I hope you fall in the ocean and drown—just like—" She broke off, tears filling her eyes, and ran past Julie from the room.

Jon rushed to Julie and threw his arms around her, burying his face in her stomach. "I like you, Julie—and I don't want you to ever go away."

Julie stooped down and drew the boy into her arms, holding him tightly. She wondered if she should cancel her date with Sean but decided against it. Emily was a confused little girl in need of counseling. Julie didn't like causing Emily distress, but at the same time she couldn't run her life according to what Emily did or did not like. Besides, the dinner with Sean was for business purposes, though of course she couldn't tell Emily that.

Julie kissed Jon's cheek, gave him another swift hug, and left the house.

❢

"So, Sean," Julie said, while trying to do justice to the baked stuffed crab she had selected from the buffet. "How long has your family lived in this area?"

"My father moved the family here from Scotland when I was a teenager. Our home had burned to the ground, and Father decided to take what money was left and join his brother here in America. My uncle is also a pastor," he said with a grimace.

"And since you've lived here have you been associated with any of the Taylors?"

His brows sailed up. "The Taylors? Must we discuss them?"

Julie shrugged, forking a spicy bite of crabmeat into her mouth before replying. "I've heard things and just wondered what your take on the family was."

"I told you." He seemed irritated as he concentrated on eating. "I've never met Jonathan Taylor, nor do I care to."

"What about his wife, Angela?" Julie asked. He looked up, and she purposely concentrated on extracting the succulent white meat from a lobster tail, dipping it in the bowl of melted butter. "I mean, I just thought you might know her, or someone from the family, since you were walking on their private beach the day I met you."

He was quiet a long time, and Julie peered up at him. His expression was uncommonly sober. "I ran across Angela a few times in past years, yes."

"And what kind of woman did she strike you as being?"

Sean shrugged. "Your typical neglected wife, I suppose. She often complained that her husband had no time for her."

"Really? You two must have been more than just acquaintances for her to confide in you like that."

A hard look glazed his blue eyes. He set down his fork and gave her his full attention. "Angela was open with everyone. She was the type who could tell a complete stranger her life story within ten minutes of meeting them. In fact, she did so the first time we met."

"And when was that?"

He leaned toward her. "And can you be tellin' me why it is you want to know?"

"Just curious." Julie made a concentrated effort to eat the food on her plate and not appear too interested in whether he responded or not. Her mock indifference paid off.

"Angela was painting a still life on the beach when I came across her the first time," Sean said at last. "An arrangement of shells. I gave her a few pointers, and we started talking. She struck me as very unhappy."

"Did she have any enemies?"

"None that I knew about."

"Hmm. And did you feel her death was a homicide—or accidental?"

"What are you—a policewoman?"

Julie shrugged. "I was just wondering. Many of the people I've run across believe Jonathan might have had something to do with her death." She folded her arms on the edge of the table and leaned on them. "What do you think?"

Sean paused to glance out the window at the calm ocean

before replying. Julie could tell he was getting impatient with her line of questioning. "She didna' get along with him, 'tis a fact. Yet for all her misery of being married to him she never complained that he was abusive toward her—physically, that is."

A measure of relief filled Julie. This was the first good thing anyone had said about Jonathan, except for Ginny.

"As to whether he killed her?" Sean lifted his hand, palm up. "Who knows? In the heat of passion anything's possible, I suppose. I wasn't in the country during the hearing, as I'd already departed to sea, so I don't know much about it. I didna' return until months later." He shifted in his chair. "Now let's talk about something else. I'm certain we can find a more pleasant subject than the Taylors."

Sean switched to a recount of one of his island visits. Julie gave him half an ear, her mind busy compiling and sorting facts. Later, the waitress came with the dessert cart, but Julie glanced at the dark sky and shook her head.

"I need to get back."

"Now?" Sean looked surprised. "What about dessert?"

"No, thanks." She scooted the chair from the table and rose. "Thank you for the meal. I enjoyed it."

He reluctantly stood but led the way to the front. After paying the bill, he took her arm and assisted her outside to where the *Bonny Lass* was docked. A full moon had risen over the dark water, lacing the waves with silver. The ride back seemed to take longer, and Julie felt relieved when the pier came into sight. Sean hopped out first then helped Julie over, but when she was on the dock, he didn't let go of her hand.

"Sean?"

Instead of replying, he pulled her close. Uneasy, she tried to pull away, but he held her firmly. Lowering his head, he kissed her. Julie broke away, embarrassed. "Why did you do that?" His kiss hadn't sparked warmth in her as Jonathan's had, but it rattled her all the same.

He chuckled. "Why would any man kiss a desirable woman?"

Instead of complimenting Julie, as he'd no doubt intended, his words infuriated her. "Good night, Sean. I can find my own way to the house."

"Julie—wait." He reached out to stop her. "Maybe I shouldn't have kissed you yet. But was it really so horrible?" He sounded confused.

Her irritation melted away, and she tried to say her words gently. "Sean, I don't want a relationship." His features stiffened, and she lifted her hands in entreaty, wishing she could make him understand. "Next to God, my career takes priority in my life, and I'd rather leave it at that. I've never been much of a dating person. Nothing personal. You do understand?"

He glanced beyond her as she spoke, then looked at her again, his eyes cold in the moon's glow. "Aye. If bein' a nanny is all you're a-wantin', then I'll leave you to that lonely life, and more's the pity. But surely you wouldna' be denying me one more wee kiss before I walk away?" His voice was a quiet growl, his brogue strong.

Without waiting for an answer, he pulled her to him, his mouth landing hard on hers with a passion that alarmed her. Just as suddenly as he grabbed her, he let go, and she almost fell off the pier and into the water. Before she could say a word, he turned and stepped into his boat. The motor started up, the boat's light flicked on, and he pulled away.

Not sure if she felt angry, hurt, violated, or all three, Julie turned—to see Jonathan standing at the foot of the pier. "Mr. Taylor!" she gasped, eyes wide. "I didn't know you were there."

"Obviously." The shadows of night played over his face, making it impossible to see his expression. Before Julie could gather her wits about her and speak, he strode off in the direction of the house.

❧

The next day Julie kept her distance from Jonathan, only speaking if spoken to. She wasn't sure what, if anything, he'd heard concerning her conversation with Sean, but she was positive he had seen the kiss. Several times during breakfast and dinner, Julie glanced Jonathan's way to see him studying her with narrowed eyes.

It was to Julie's complete astonishment when he appeared at the playroom door the following day, leaned against the frame, and suggested an outing for all four of them.

Emily's eyes widened in surprise, and Jon popped up off the floor like a jack-in-the-box. "Really, Daddy?" he asked in amazement. A day with their father was obviously not a common occurrence in the children's lives.

"Yes, Jon," he said, showing more tolerance to the boy than usual. "I think it's time Miss Rae saw some of the sights."

Jon's eyes brightened. "Can we take her to the lighthouse?"

"That sounds like a good idea. It takes awhile to get there, though, so we should be making tracks soon." Jonathan turned his attention to Julie. "Well?"

"It's almost lunchtime," Julie said, strangely nervous. "We can't go anywhere until the children have their lunch. Mrs. Leighton wouldn't approve."

One brow lifted in amusement. "I'll have Mrs. Ruggles pack a hamper. We'll eat in the countryside."

The next few minutes were a blur to Julie as she helped the children find appropriate clothes, then changed into jeans and a cocoa-and-blue striped pullover top. Why the sudden turnaround? Why was Jonathan seeking out her company? And why was she so eagerly anticipating a day in his?

Once assembled, they headed to the garage where Clancy was putting a coat of wax on Angela's Corvette. "We'll dispense with the Rolls today and take the Lincoln," Jonathan said. "I assume the gas tank is full?"

"Yes, Sir," Clancy said in a deferential tone. Only by the hardness in his eyes could Julie see that Jonathan had an enemy in his chauffeur. "I'll just run up and change," he said, putting down the can of wax and heading to his apartment over the garage.

"No need for that. I won't be requiring your services today."

"Of course, Mr. Taylor." A muscle in Clancy's jaw worked, but he turned away before Jonathan could see the hate marring his face. Only Julie saw, but then she was looking for it.

The day was cloudy, but no rain loomed in the forecast, and the drive was pleasant. Jonathan seemed unusually conversant, pointing out historical markers and places of interest. On the other hand, the children were quiet, apparently uncertain how to respond to their father's gregarious behavior.

Settling back, Julie enjoyed the view. White pines and maples blanketed the countryside, filling the rolling land with greenery. Julie was charmed to see a white-steepled church nestled on a hill, amid the towering evergreens. It would look just like a scene from a nostalgic Christmas card when there was snow.

An hour into the drive, Jon spoke for the first time, claiming he needed to go to the bathroom. After a quick stop at a gas station they were soon on their way again.

When they arrived at the rocky promontory where the famous Portland Head Light sat, Julie gave a gasp of delight. The lighthouse and its surrounding buildings were painted ivory, the roofs of the buildings brick red. The charming structure sat on a bed of moss atop a massive gray rock. But what struck Julie was how small it all was in comparison with the mighty Atlantic. The sea's crested waves crashed with fury upon the rock where the lighthouse perched, as if trying to reach and destroy the conical fortress that had long aided ships at sea.

Julie leaned against the white rail, looking far below. Jonathan's sudden presence beside her startled her, and she turned curious eyes his way. Strands of dark hair blew over his forehead, tossed by strong gusts of wind—which was more prominent here with no trees to block its passage.

"It's been said that when Longfellow was a boy, he would sit at the base over there, next to the lighthouse, and stare out to sea," Jonathan said, motioning to the sturdy structure with a slight nod of his head. "When he was older he wrote a poem about this place. According to the brochure, George Washington authorized its construction, and two masons hauled the stones to this spot by oxen. The lighthouse was first lit with whale oil in 1791, and in all that time the tower has remained intact, warning ships at sea, though it's fully automated now and doesn't require a lighthouse keeper to live on the premises."

"You know so much about it." Julie looked at the tower with fascination. The children stood at the base, their little hands on the edifice, their heads tilted back as far as they could go.

Julie pondered the structure. Jesus was a lot like that tower. Faithful, strong, capable—a mighty fortress in the midst of storms. And like the lighthouse did during the dark of night and in murky fog, Jesus shone forth His beacon of light to aid others in what direction to go when storms beat down on them.

Julie turned her gaze toward the vast ocean. It seemed overpowering, a formidable foe. Yet one small beam of light directed into the darkness could make all the difference and save a ship from being smashed onto the rocks—but more important it could save lives.

Pensive, Julie glanced at Jonathan then out to sea again. She was convinced that the only way for healing to begin in this man and his children was to uncover the entire truth concerning what really happened the night Angela died. Lies and half-truths were grounded in darkness. And no one could survive for long in darkness.

"You're a million miles away," Jonathan said softly. "What were you thinking?"

Julie started in surprise and turned to meet his steady gaze. "I was thinking about light breaking through darkness."

"Light breaking through darkness?" he repeated, as though he hadn't heard her correctly.

She nodded. "Sometimes I think people can be caught in a pit of darkness made up of lies and the inability to see truth. Harsh memories can also aid that darkness, especially when they're relived continually. Nothing can grow without light.

Without it, things become stagnant. People become stagnant."

"My, but you're philosophical today," Jonathan mused.

She tilted her head. "Tell me, why did you leave the church? Why did you walk away from the very people who could have supported you through the difficult times?"

His features stiffened. "I would prefer not to discuss this." He gazed back out at the ocean. His hands clutched the railing until his knuckles showed white.

Julie let out a small, resigned breath. "Okay, I'll quit, but first I want to say one more thing."

"I suppose I can't stop you," he said, irritated.

Julie regarded him, her voice gentle. "Just remember: When you turn your back to the light you can't see to go forward. And each step you take away from it plunges you into greater darkness. But when you face the light your path is clear. And each step you take toward it, the more brilliant your surroundings become."

He turned his head to look at her. His eyes were unreadable, and Julie wished she knew what he was thinking.

The children scampered up to them, full of questions, the excitement of the lighthouse obviously overriding their earlier hesitancy to talk. Jonathan patiently answered each one, though Julie could tell he seemed preoccupied, and several times throughout the rest of their visit she caught him staring at her.

On the drive back they parked at a roadside stop and ate roast beef sandwiches. An elderly couple with Alabama license plates on their car slowed beside them and asked directions to the Wadsworth-Longfellow House. Jonathan pointed down the road, and the man nodded and smiled. "Nice family you got there, Mister," he said looking first at Julie, then at Jon sitting on her lap and Emily on the bench next to her.

The man drove away. Jonathan's and Julie's eyes met across the picnic table, and Julie found it hard to take her next breath. Averting her gaze, she abruptly set Jon on the ground and stood. "I think we should be getting back. Don't you?"

"It is getting late," Jonathan agreed in a low voice. The

ride back was quiet. When they reached the house, the children piled out of the car and ran to the building in a race to see who could get there first. Julie noted Mrs. Leighton opening the back door, as if she'd been watching for them, and Julie put one foot on the ground to follow.

"Go for a walk with me?" Jonathan asked. "Mrs. Leighton can take care of the kids for a few minutes." His gray eyes entreated her, and she nodded, feeling both caution and excitement that he should ask her.

They picked their way along the path that wound alongside the rocky cliff. The screeching gulls provided background noise to the frequent sound of splashing water hitting rocks.

"Thank you for all you've done for the children," Jonathan said. "They seem to have accepted you."

A frown creased Julie's brow. "Not Emily. And I'm not sure she ever will, though I've tried to be her friend."

His hand on her arm stopped her. Surprised, she faced him.

"You're wrong. I've never seen her so amiable with anyone. The two nannies the agency sent before I hired you had to seek her out every day. She hid from them," he explained. "But Emily sticks to you like glue."

Julie considered that. She'd always thought the girl's behavior in that respect strange, given Emily's animosity toward her. "I've come to care for her a great deal. Her and Jon both."

"And what about me, Julie?" he asked softly, using her given name for the first time and sending delightful tremors shivering through her. His finger stroked her cheek. "Could you learn to care for me, as well?"

"I—" Julie stood with slightly parted lips, unable to form any other words.

"Julie." He said the word as though in a caress. Cupping her face in his hand, he slowly inclined his head, and time ceased to exist.

Reason broke through the cloud of pleasure engulfing Julie and reminded her of the folly of getting involved with this man. She stepped backward, breaking the kiss.

"Please, don't—I—I can't—"

Bitterness replaced the softness in his eyes. "What's wrong? Aren't I as good as MacPhearson? Your kiss said you thought so anyway."

Her jaw dropped as understanding dawned, and she clenched her hands at her sides. "Just for the record, I'm not some sort of prize to be obtained by you or Sean. I'm a woman with feelings, and I refuse to stand in the middle of some juvenile tug-of-war between two egotistical males who act more like little boys than men! So put that in your pipe and smoke it!" she retorted, using one of her father's old phrases.

Spinning on her heel, Julie marched back to the house. She couldn't remember ever being so angry. Hurt. Humiliated. The episode with Sean seemed mild in comparison. But then he'd never touched her heart as Jonathan had.

Footsteps crunched behind her, and he grasped her arm gently. "Wait—please. What I said was totally uncalled for." Remorse tinged his voice. "I apologize."

Julie turned, flicking a glance upward.

"Forgive me?" he asked.

She nodded but didn't smile. "I should get back to the children." This time when she walked away, he didn't stop her. Glancing over her shoulder, Julie saw him facing the sea, his broad shoulders slumped, his head down.

Ignoring the cry of her heart, she increased her pace toward the house before she did something stupid—like turn around and run back to him and into his arms.

☙

Julie sat on the hood of the car near the wharf, tossing bread crumbs to hungry gulls and watching the everyday hubbub of life on a seaport. Owners of vessels docked at the harbor conversed with one another and cleaned and repaired boats and sails. Fishing boats dotted the blue horizon, and to Julie's left a pile of empty lobster traps littered the deck.

Confused about the feelings she had for Jonathan, Julie put off returning to the Taylor home. Needing counsel, she had sought Pastor MacPhearson's advice after church. He had only been able to spare her five minutes but had shown concern, praying with Julie for God to show her wisdom.

"You look as if the weight of the world is resting on your shoulders, Boss-lady," a teasing male voice said near her ear.

Shocked, Julie started, dropping the sack of stale bread crumbs. Whirling around, she faced the newcomer. "Dale!" she cried happily, giving her friend and operative a quick hug. "I never expected you here! I thought by now you'd started your posh new job."

The short, sandy-haired man gave her one of his carefree grins, shrugging muscular shoulders. "I explained the situation to the D.A. and asked for more time. I couldn't leave you in the thick of things, now could I? Speaking of which, how is the case progressing?"

Julie groaned. "It's not. Get in the car, and we'll talk."

He opened the passenger door and picked up the stack of books on the upholstered seat. Glancing at the top one, he then looked Julie's way.

Her face grew warm. "That's for the kids I've been hired to watch. A book of Bible stories. I ordered it on the web," she explained as she started the car.

"And the Nancy Drew and Trixie Belden mysteries underneath?" he inquired, his lips twitching in amusement.

"I checked them out from the library the other day. I thought Emily might like to read them."

"Emily, huh?"

"Just get in, Dale." She felt herself blush.

Dale didn't say another word but moved the books to the backseat and climbed inside. Once they were on their way, Julie glanced at him. "Have you uncovered anything?"

"A mountain load. I have some information on the Taylor staff which I think you'll find highly interesting."

"Let's hear it."

"Were you aware that one Bessie Lou Kotter brought sexual harassment charges against her two former male employers in

Louisiana, though word has it they rejected her advances?"
Julie shook her head, and Dale continued, "There was talk of a
torrid love affair—at least that's how the neighbor put it—
between Bessie Lou and Bryce Colby, a lawyer she kept house
for. But when his wife found out, everything hit the fan. Bessie
Lou lost her job and moved north to stay with her cousin—
in Maine."

Julie's brow furrowed. "Interesting. When I talked to her at
the ice cream parlor she seemed upset that Jonathan hadn't
been convicted for Angela's death. A woman spurned?"

Dale nodded. "Could be. But it's still speculation."

Julie sighed. "Yeah, you're right."

"But the news about the chauffeur, Ron Clancy, is more
than speculation," he added, a teasing note to his voice.

When he didn't say anything further, Julie pulled the car to
the side of the road and faced him. "Look, Dale, I'm in no
mood for your games right now. Just tell me what you know."

His brow furrowed in curious concern. "Hey, you're really
wound up tight. The kids or the case?"

"A little of both, I guess." Julie let out a long sigh. "Watching those kids takes up more time than I would have ever
believed possible! I haven't been able to do much in the
detecting department, except for questioning the staff and
doing some snooping around the house. But when I do get a
concrete lead, it usually winds up a dead end." She looked at
him. "So tell me about Clancy."

"Six years ago, he did ten months in a Texas state prison
on charges of blackmail, and get this—attempted murder.
And it wasn't his first time in front of a judge."

Julie chewed her lip. "Why did he serve such a short sen-
tence?"

Dale shrugged. "You know how the system works, Jules.
He got out on a technicality. His sister hired some sleazy
lawyer who knew how to find the loopholes and took his
case to the court of appeals."

Julie nodded, her mouth grim. "Anything else?"

"Mrs. Leighton, the housekeeper, came with Angela as a package deal when she married Jonathan. But what isn't common knowledge is that Mrs. Leighton is Angela's aunt."

"What?!" Julie's eyes widened.

Dale nodded. "Apparently no love was lost among family members, but the old biddy had a fond spot in her heart for her wayward niece and followed her to Maine."

"Wayward?"

"Angela got pregnant before she married. Fooled around with her sister's boyfriend behind her back."

"Jonathan," Julie breathed, closing her eyes.

"Jonathan," Dale affirmed. "Claire Vanderhoff and Jonathan Taylor were engaged to be married."

Julie suddenly felt dizzy, and Dale put a hand on her arm. "You okay?"

She vaguely nodded. "It sounds a lot like a daytime soap opera, doesn't it?" Her voice came out funny, and she cleared her throat. "I find it interesting that Claire Vanderhoff kept that information to herself. I can't wait to hear her excuse why."

She furrowed her brow. "But something doesn't gel. If Mrs. Leighton cared for Angela, why would she stay at the house with someone suspected of Angela's murder? And why would she work as the hired help if she was family?"

Dale shrugged. "The children, maybe? They're all that's left of Angela. As to the other, Mrs. Leighton owned a maid's service before Jonathan and Angela married. She sold it afterward and, my guess is, offered her niece her services."

"Hmm. That makes sense." Julie tapped her fingers on the wheel. "What about Mrs. Ruggles, the cook? I rarely see the woman, but I know she visits someone in town on her days off."

Dale nodded. "She was hired on after Angela died. She has a lame sister in town and visits her on Sundays. And Shannon Lassiter, the new maid, is distantly related to another girl who worked at the Taylors' years ago—a cousin—but she left before the drowning. Shannon is studying to be an actress."

"An actress, huh?" The girl did tend to be overly dramatic at times. "So where do we go from here?"

"I thought I'd get an apartment in town. I could be there if you need me, when you need me."

Shocked, Julie darted a glance his way. "Why, Dale? Why would you do that when you've got a better paying job waiting in the wings?"

"You shouldn't have to ask that, Boss. Your dad gave me a head start in the business when I was no more than an eager kid still wet behind the ears. I'll never forget that."

Julie smiled at him. She and Dale had always been close, like brother and sister. They'd tried dating once, but some relationships just weren't meant to be. They got along better keeping their relationship on a friends-only basis.

A thought struck her. "I have an idea. I heard the staff talking this morning and apparently Jonathan is looking for a gardener. The last one was fired a few days ago. You did some landscaping in high school, didn't you?"

Dale nodded, catching on. "Yeah, though it's been awhile since I handled a spade. I guess I'll need to check out a book at the library dealing with the vegetation of the area. Plant life here is different than down south. I'll do that tomorrow."

His eyebrows lifted. "Do I come recommended or on my own?"

Julie deliberated, staring out the windshield. "I think we should be strangers. My job is tenuous—I'm on a probationary period—so my word probably wouldn't be regarded highly. And staff doesn't last long there, so be on your guard." She threw him a warning look. "No funny business, Dale. Keep everything above-board. I don't want to have to bail you out of jail yet too."

"Who me?" He grinned like an errant schoolboy. "Okay, gotcha, Boss. If you'll drop me off at my hotel, I'll get right to work."

ten

The weeks at the Taylor residence passed with barely a ripple to disturb the peace. Dale was hired on and given the room next to Clancy's. He did his job well, keeping his eyes and ears open and searching out clues in his spare time.

Several times a week he and Julie risked a few minutes of being seen together to compare notes and share any new information. On Sundays they went to town for church, talking freely on the drive there and back. Dale had never been a churchgoer, and Julie wasn't sure if he knew Jesus as his personal Savior. But the opportunity to discuss the case was too good for him to pass up, and he agreed to her invitation each time, though rather reluctantly.

Emily was less morose, though by no stretch of the imagination could she be labeled a happy child. She was, as Jonathan had called her, "amiable." And Jon, as always, was his sweet self, bringing love to everyone around him, though he had his mischievous moments too.

But the change in Jonathan was the real surprise. He seemed like a different person—seeking out Julie's company often and showing a gentle side Julie hadn't known existed. They were now on a first-name basis and often walked together along the rocky coast, sometimes not saying a word, other times conversing freely. Jonathan opened up to Julie in ways she never would have imagined, though he said nothing about Angela or her death. Nor had he tried to kiss her again. Julie told herself she was relieved about this, but what she felt was annoyingly far from relief.

She strolled between the garden hedges while mulling over the past weeks in his company. Jonathan was out of town on business, and the children were with their tutor, an elderly professor-type who recently had returned to the mansion and resumed lessons. Julie looked at the forest of trees flanking the garden, feeling restless. She had just decided to go jogging when Dale appeared around the corner, garden tools in hand. He knelt on the ground a few feet away, though still within hearing distance.

"I found Dan Fielder," he said quietly.

It took every bit of willpower for Julie to stay calm and show no expression on her face, in case anyone might be watching. She walked closer to the house, bent over, and plucked a purple Shasta daisy from the ground. "And?"

"He lives about fifty miles from here. When his agency went bankrupt, he moved to another town to start over in another line of work. Manages a hardware store now. I met him and told him I'm investigating the Taylor case. He was glad to help."

Julie blew out an exasperated breath, waiting. "And?"

"Jonathan Taylor had a private eye—Dan Fielder—trail his wife after receiving several anonymous and revealing letters about her extracurricular activities. It seems the little lady wasn't too happy with staying home to nest."

"Daa–ale," Julie said in a warning tone.

He grinned as he dug in the dirt with the trowel. "Okay, okay, Boss. Angela was involved in several affairs with other men. While Jonathan went out of town on business trips, his wife went on the prowl."

Julie crushed the flower in her hand, feeling as if something had crushed her heart. She remembered Jonathan's behavior after they'd returned from their outing to the lighthouse and he had thrown Sean's name in her face. And Julie wasn't even special to him. How would Jonathan react if the woman he loved were to get involved with another man? Angry enough to kill? Memory of the day he destroyed Angela's portrait and the bitter words he had spoken came to Julie.

"Hey, Jules. You okay? You look pale," Dale said. Julie managed a nod, and his hazel eyes filled with sympathy. "You really have it bad, don't you?"

She looked away. "I don't know what you mean."

"Come on, Boss. My job is detecting, remember? And it doesn't take a whole lotta clues to see you're in love with the suspect."

"He's not a suspect," Julie said between her teeth. "Innocent until proven guilty—isn't that how the term goes? Or have the rules changed without my knowledge? We're supposed to be looking for proof as to what happened here over a year ago, Dale. Not supporting rumors. And besides, all charges against Jonathan were dropped at the hearing, due to inconclusive evidence."

"But we know better now, don't we? The man had his wife trailed. She was unfaithful to him. The night she died they had a terrible argument. It doesn't look too good to me."

Julie turned away at his low spoken words and took a few steps, her hands clenched at her sides.

"Look out!"

The breath was knocked from her as Dale tackled her from behind. Sharp corners of the flagstones painfully scraped her hands and forearms when she hit the ground. Her chin struck the pavement. Milliseconds later a thunderous crash splintered the air as a heavy urn broke into pieces on the very spot where Julie had been standing.

She looked in horror at the jagged shards of broken pottery, then upward to the second story window where a curtain fluttered.

But there was no wind.

"You okay?" Dale breathed.

He barely waited for Julie's nod and ran for the house. Before he could gain entrance and try to catch the culprit, Jonathan hurried out of the door, his eyes wide with shock.

"What's going on? Julie! Are you okay?" His words sounded raspy, as if he'd run far. "Mr. Greenly! What is the meaning of this?"

Dale stood there, obviously wanting to run upstairs, judging from the way his gaze kept roaming to the balcony.

"Julie was almost killed." He motioned to the shattered urn. "That came a hairsbreadth from landing on top of her head."

Alarm filled Jonathan's eyes. "I'm sure it was an accident."

"Mr. Taylor, with all due respect, four-foot urns don't pick themselves up off the ground and jump off the balcony rail. What happened here was intentional," Dale said, his expression grim. "Someone had to pick up that urn. Now if you'll excuse me, I'm going to try to find out who." He ran into the house without waiting for a reply.

Another wave of dizziness struck Julie as she tried to rise, Dale's ominous words hitting home. Someone had tried to kill her? Why? Was her cover blown? And where had Jonathan suddenly come from?

He rushed to her side. "Are you all right?"

She gave a vague nod, unable to articulate any words. Frowning, he lifted her bleeding chin tenderly, eyeing it, then took her hands and examined the scraped palms and inside of her arms. "Let's get you in the house." His hands were gentle as he helped her up.

"I thought you were out of town," Julie managed to say.

"I came back a day early. Now that negotiations have progressed concerning the strike, I probably won't have to leave here as often."

"Oh." She attempted a smile but knew she must have fallen short when she saw concern fill Jonathan's eyes again. Why did he always seem to be in the wrong place at the wrong time? How could she convince others of his innocence when he never had a good alibi? When his actions didn't just point to guilt—but loudly proclaimed it? Yet prove his innocence she must. Otherwise she had fallen in love with a murderer.

Avoiding his searching gaze, Julie felt as though the urn really had broken over her head and she might pass out. Dale was right. She loved this man. She had been avoiding it for weeks, but there it was. She loved him.

"Julie, are you all right?" Before she could answer, Jonathan swept her up into his arms. "You must have hit your head when you fell. You look positively shaken."

"I'm. . .okay." Her words came out disjointed.

"You don't look okay," he insisted as he carried her toward the back entrance. "You need tending to, and we should call a doctor to examine you and make sure you didn't suffer a concussion."

"Don't you think you should call the police first, Mr. Taylor?" Dale asked quietly from the doorway.

Startled, Julie turned her gaze to him. Dale observed them, his look sober, questioning, but not all that surprised. Julie felt Jonathan's muscles tense, and she pulled her arm away from where it was looped around his neck.

"Please, I can walk," she insisted.

Jonathan ignored her. "You're right, Mr. Greenly. The police should be notified. See to it. I'll tend to Miss Rae."

Jonathan carried her into the house. As they moved past Dale, Julie's eyes met her operative's. She'd known him long enough to interpret that look. *He's the prime suspect, Julie. Accept the truth.*

Closing her eyes, she refused to believe what logic told her must be true. In her heart she knew it wasn't so.

❧

Julie sat alone in the sunroom, though dark night had long ago fallen. Her gaze went to the huge yellowish-white moon that shed pale light through the eastern windows. The two police officers and the doctor had left long ago, and Julie mulled over the previous few hours. Uncomfortable, she fidgeted.

In her heart she was determined to believe Jonathan's innocence, but Dale's words stabbed her mind like poisonous wasp stings. Dale had always been one of her best operatives, someone she trusted implicitly, someone whose ideas and opinions she highly valued. And what was even more disconcerting— he was usually right in his assumptions.

When Officer Bryant asked Jonathan where he had been at the time the urn fell, Jonathan looked uneasy then admitted he was in his bedroom, unpacking a few things from his briefcase. The fact that Jonathan's bedroom was close to the room with the balcony where the urn had fallen wasn't in his favor. Nor was the fact that he hadn't seen or heard anything unusual, either before or after the incident.

At the time Julie sloughed it off, her mind still wrapped up in the tender way Jonathan had cleaned her wounds. Afterward, to her absolute shock, he kissed her scraped palms, much as he might do for Emily, though the look in his eyes was anything but paternal. Even now the memory of his intimate gesture made her tingle with warmth.

"Oh, dear God, give me wisdom in this situation," Julie whispered, lowering her forehead into one hand.

"Miss Julie?"

The soft voice coming so suddenly from the dark made Julie start. She turned to where Emily stood several feet away dressed in her long pink satin nightgown and slippers. The child stepped closer. In the moon's glow Julie could see the uncertainty that clouded her face. Her eyes were anxious.

"Is something wrong, Emily?"

A single tear slipped down her cheek, as forlorn and lonely as its small owner. Emily swiped it away with a knuckled fist. She straightened her shoulders in an attempt at courage, but her voice wavered when she spoke. "Are they going to take my daddy away again?"

Julie's heart constricted. "No—of course not. He didn't do anything wrong."

Emily sucked in her lower lip, obviously trying to hold on to what little control she possessed. "Did someone try to kill you? Is that why the doctor and the police came? I heard Miss Shannon and Mrs. Leighton talking about it in the kitchen."

Julie deliberated between glossing over the truth and telling an outright lie to placate the girl's fears. Remember-ing the conversation she'd had with Emily months ago about lying, she nodded and gave a quiet "yes" instead.

Emily bit her trembling lip. "I'm scared."

Julie held out her arms, and Emily flew into them, clutching her around the waist. The tears fell in earnest. "I didn't mean what I said about h–hoping you would drown. I was just mad. Please, Miss Julie. D–don't let anything bad happen to Jon or me. P–please?"

"I would never let anyone hurt either of you," Julie said as she stroked the girl's hair and held her close for a few minutes while she calmed down. "But, Emily—" She pulled away to look into her eyes. "If you've been holding anything back, you must tell me. No more secrets. Okay?"

Emily stiffened, and Julie thought she would break away and run from the room. But she gave a vague nod instead.

Glad Emily had grown to trust her enough to come to her, Julie took her hands and squeezed them. "Remember when I told you that Jesus wants to be your friend for always and how He's there when you're lonely or scared?"

The little girl nodded.

"Well, it helps me feel better when I pray. And I think you also might feel better if you pray and ask Him to take care of you and Jon and your father and help all of you through this. Would you like to do that, Emily? Would you like to ask Jesus to be your forever friend?"

"Yes," Emily whispered.

"Then ask Him to. Right here and now. It's okay. Just talk to Him like you would to anyone else."

Emily paused then squeezed her eyes shut. "Mr. Jesus— will You please be my forever friend? I read the stories about You in that book Miss Julie bought, and I want to be Your friend too. And could You please keep us safe from being killed, like You did for Daniel and Esther and King David and Paul—and all those other people in the stories I read? Thank You, Mr. Jesus."

She opened her eyes, and her lips turned up in a hopeful smile. "Did I do it right? Do you think He heard me?"

"Oh, I know He did, Emily," Julie murmured, tears washing her eyes. "And you said it perfectly."

She drew the child close for a hug, and Emily didn't object.

Three days later, Julie sat on the playroom floor with the children. Shannon bustled through the open doorway with the lunch tray. Julie looked up from peering over Emily's shoulder as the child drew a barren landscape with leafless trees in her sketchpad. Since the night in the sunroom, relations between Emily and Julie had altered dramatically.

"Mmm. Do I smell Chicken Florentine?" Julie asked.

"That's my favorite," Emily said, throwing down her charcoal pencil.

Jon tossed aside his picture book and was the first to be seated at the plastic children's table where they often ate their lunches.

"Sorry I'm late, Miss Rae," Shannon said, out of breath, her eyes sparkling with something akin to triumph. "But Dale came by the kitchen to talk. He helped me set the trays."

"That's nice." Julie took Jon's roll off the blue divided plate and buttered it, refusing to play the silly game in which Shannon tried to rope her. Shannon was the type who took pleasure in trying to steal other women's boyfriends. Ever since Jonathan had shown an interest in Julie, Shannon flirted with him at every opportunity, though he seemed oblivious to the fact. After the attempt on Julie's life, Dale checked on Julie several times that evening. Shannon then concentrated her efforts on him, obviously thinking Julie and Dale had something going. Julie pitied the girl, who seemed to feel the need to hurt others in order to build up her ego.

"I hope you don't mind," Shannon said, her expression showing she could care less. "About Dale coming to talk to me, I mean."

"Not at all."

Frowning at her unsuccessful attempt to get a rise out of Julie, Shannon finally left. Relieved, Julie took hold of the children's hands and offered a prayer for the food. Before eating, she took the napkin from her tray to lay it in her lap. She noticed a tiny corner of yellow peeking from beneath her large wheat roll, which sat on its own saucer. Julie waited until the children's attention was diverted before snatching the message and slipping it in her pocket to read later.

Almost two hours passed before she found an opportunity to duck in her room, lock the door and fish the note from her pocket.

Meet me at the pier tonight after the kids are in bed.
D.

Julie grew thoughtful as she crumpled the paper into a tiny ball and flushed it down the toilet. Dale must have learned something. Otherwise he would never take the chance of blowing their cover by sending her the note. As she left the bathroom, Julie glanced toward the dresser and froze. Propped against the mirror, another message demanded attention.

She walked across the room, snatched up the business-sized blank envelope, and pulled out a piece of paper. Large letters cut from a magazine screamed their message. The note was brief and to the point.

The other day was only a warning. Leave and you will be spared. Stay—and you will die.

Julie tried to swallow, but her throat was dry. How different this threat was from Emily's childish warning scrawled on the mirror in Firelight Red lipstick months ago! But Julie knew the little girl wasn't behind the dirty work this time. The note, though chilling and obviously the creation of a disturbed mind, was far too sophisticated to be anything Emily could fabricate. Besides which, Emily had opened up to Julie, even showing her the excellent, if gloomy, drawings from her sketchbook and joining Julie and Jon in their games. But Emily still hadn't told her any secrets she might be hiding.

Julie stuffed the vicious message back into its envelope and stuck it in her pocket to show Dale later.

Later seemed a long time in coming, but at last the children were bedded for the night, with hugs and kisses given, and Julie went to her room to change into a sweat suit. If asked where she was going after dark, she would say she needed a run, which was the absolute truth.

Strangely, after the police questioning on the evening someone had tried to kill her, Jonathan had made himself scarce, holing himself up in his office every day. At mealtimes, a worried frown marred his brow, and he scarcely ate anything offered. He acted distant, almost cold—a complete turnaround from their closeness of past weeks.

Something was bothering him, and Julie was afraid to probe too deeply to discover what. Memory of his words concerning God, that he'd spoken the first time he'd left for a business trip, haunted Julie. "I sincerely doubt He'd want anything to do with a sinner like me," he had said, his eyes filled with self-loathing. As if a heavy sin weighed upon his heart.

"No!" Julie said aloud, tying her sneakers with angry little jerks. "I refuse to believe he did it!" Grabbing her jacket, she left the room and crept downstairs and out the front door, glad when no one appeared to ask questions.

❧

"Pheww!" Dale gave a low whistle. "You're definitely not on someone's popularity list." He handed the threatening note back to Julie then turned off his flashlight. Inky darkness again surrounded them, with only the faint glow of the three-quarter moon, hovering over the black ocean, giving off light.

"I can't understand it," Julie said with a moan. "I've been so careful not to blow my cover, only proceeding with the investigation when I was sure I wasn't being observed. But someone obviously knows I'm here as more than a nanny."

"Or not."

Julie looked at his dim form. "What do you mean?"

"That might not be the reason you've been targeted." Dale was silent a moment as if struggling with what he wanted to say. "You know, Jules, maybe you should bow out of this investigation and head back home. I mean, think about it—you're the one being threatened here—whatever the reason."

Julie shook her head. "No way! A Daniels never quits when the going gets tough."

"But a Daniels has never been the target for murder either. It wouldn't be cowardly of you to give this up and tell that Vanderhoff woman to find someone else. No one would think any less of you." He was quiet as he studied her.

"And another thing," he said more softly, "I think maybe your heart's overpowering your head right now, and it's clouding your logic."

Julie frowned. "And what's that supposed to mean?"

"I've never seen you act anything but the cool professional, especially when the pressure's on. But just the wrong mention of Jonathan Taylor's name sets you off like a lioness fighting for her cub. Only I'm afraid you're the one who's going to get mauled in all this, Jules."

She whirled around and stalked a few steps away from him, her hands clenched at her sides. "Thanks for the advice and concern, Dale. But I assure you it's unwarranted. Jonathan Taylor did not murder his wife. And he didn't try to do me in either!"

She spun to face him again, her hands going up in a pleading gesture. "Don't ask me to explain—I can't. I'll admit that at times I've thought him as guilty as you so obviously do. But certain things just don't gel."

"Like?"

Julie let out a breath, stuffing her hands into the pockets of her jacket. "Okay. Like the fact that he became a Christian a few months before his wife's death."

Dale shrugged. "I can't speak from experience, Jules, but even Christians mess up, don't they? And if he was really angry, he could've put that hole in the boat in the heat of the moment."

"Yes, I suppose," Julie agreed, "but I don't believe that about Jonathan. Sometimes there's this look in his eyes—"

Dale gave a disbelieving grunt, but Julie ignored him and continued, "There's this look in his eyes of terrible sadness, as if he were the victim in all this."

"Boss, I'm surprised at you. A look? You're judging your assessment based on a look?"

Julie crossed her arms and stared him down, even though she couldn't see him well. "Yes. Coupled with this gut feeling I've had almost since I came here. Jonathan Taylor did not, nor has he ever tried to, murder anyone—and I'll scrounge up every bit of hard evidence I can to prove it!"

The tide coming in and splashing against the pilings was the only sound as the two faced in a standoff. At last Dale relaxed and uncrossed his arms. "Okay, okay. I know better than to disprove that gut feeling of yours. It's never been wrong before—but there could be a first time. Just don't get careless. You're obviously on someone's hit list."

Dale's words took the starch out of Julie's back, and she slumped. Remembering that she still didn't know why Dale had appointed this meeting, Julie asked dully, "Why the note, Dale?"

"Two things. I dug up some info on Sean MacPhearson, like you asked. Were you aware he left the area and sailed away on his yacht—yes, he had a yacht—the morning after Angela drowned?"

"Really?" Interested, Julie lifted her brow.

"Care to know the name of the vessel?"

"Enlighten me," she said, though she could guess.

"The *Angel Dawn*. Ten to one, Angela's middle name is Dawn."

Julie thought back to the bios. "It is. Anything else?"

"All that day and into the night, Sean was seen in town and at a local bar with friends. One of them dropped Sean off at his yacht late that night."

"That doesn't mean he couldn't have knocked the hole in the boat earlier," Julie argued.

"But for what motive? He had no legal ties to Angela to

get any of her money."

"What if money wasn't the motive? What if they had a lovers' spat—assuming they were an item?"

"I don't think so. Sean doesn't seem the type. If Angela did threaten to dump him, I see him as trying to win her back—not eliminating her. He had nothing to gain by her death."

"Maybe." Remembering Sean's angry kiss at this very pier, Julie grew pensive. "But then again, maybe not. Let's not write Sean off yet. He gets hotheaded at times."

"I'll keep looking into it," Dale assured her. "Also, I've been buddying up with Clancy. The man's definitely hiding something—and I'm willing to bet it isn't good. Tomorrow he's leaving for the day to see his brother, and I'm going to take that opportunity to look around his place and see what I can find."

"You mean breaking and entering, don't you?" Julie asked, a warning note in her voice. "You know how I feel about that, Dale. The last thing I need is to bail you out of jail. And you certainly don't need to jeopardize your job here either."

"Jules, we can't play the nice guys anymore. I know that since you became a Christian your values have changed. And, believe it or not, I think the change is great. You're like a different person—not to say you weren't nice before," he added. "But detecting is our job. And unfortunately the bad guys don't just walk up to us and turn themselves in. We have to catch them. And sometimes that means bending the rules a little."

He put his hands to her shoulders. "Face it, Jules—we're talking murder here. And it could've been yours."

Closing her eyes, Julie shivered. Dale was right. She still didn't like the idea of him "bending the rules," but human life was in the balance. The children might be in danger. Weren't there exceptions to the rules in such extenuating circumstances?

"As soon as you can, let me know what you find." Turning, she left the privacy of the cove and made her way back to the house, the glow of her flashlight bouncing off the rocky path before her.

eleven

Two days. Julie tried to focus on her book of devotions but ended up slamming the hardback shut. She set the book down and walked out into the backyard and the sculptured garden, playing nervously with the zipper of her windbreaker. It had been two days since she and Dale had talked.

She assumed everything had gone smoothly and he hadn't been caught. Yesterday had been Dale's day off, and Julie had been so sure he would contact her and let her know of his findings as soon as he returned from wherever he went. But he hadn't. And now it was another day, and no one seemed to know where he was.

Julie turned on the stone path, inhaling sharply when she came face-to-face with Jonathan.

"I was hoping I'd run into you. Is everything okay?" His eyes studied her.

Julie nodded and forced herself to stop playing with her zipper. "Just restless."

"Are the children taking their lessons with Mr. Taggart?"

Julie again nodded.

"Take a walk with me?" he asked softly.

Feeling as if she could drown in the silvery-gray pools of his eyes, she forced herself to take a step backward. "I— uh—not right now."

"What's wrong?"

"Nothing." She averted her gaze and focused on a climbing rhododendron bush covering the rock wall of the house.

"Then why are you so distant all of a sudden? I'd thought—"

"Me distant?" Julie interrupted in surprise. "I'm not the one who locked myself in an office for almost a week." Instantly she wished she could retrieve the telling words.

Jonathan smiled. "I'm sorry about that. I had pressing business that couldn't be ignored."

"For five full days?"

Jonathan's smile faded. "It couldn't be helped."

Julie looked away, embarrassed by her behavior. "I'm sorry, Jonathan. I had no right. I've had a lot on my mind. I— I think I should get back to the house now. I promised the kids a game of Parcheesi after their lessons." She began to walk away.

"Their lessons don't end for another two hours."

"Oh. Well, I have things I need to do."

"Julie?"

Against her better judgment she faced him, trying to remain aloof. Yet the tender look in his eyes threatened her firm resolve. He covered the space between them.

"I'll admit I've kept my distance, but not because of anything you've done. I've been thinking a lot this past week— about us." His hand lifted to stroke her cheek with the back of his knuckles, and her heart began to race. "You're the best thing that's happened to this place," he murmured, his voice husky. "You have a brightness about you that draws people like bees to a honeycomb. I don't know yet what it is about you, Julie Rae, but I'd like the chance to find out. To learn everything there is to know about you and who you are."

As he spoke, he lowered his head, and at his last words his lips brushed hers in a kiss that almost robbed Julie of common sense. Almost.

She put her hands to his shoulders and took a shaky step backward, attempting to get on solid footing again. "Don't, Jonathan—I can't."

His brows drew downward. "Why not?"

"I just can't. There's so much I want to tell you—someday," she said, trying to communicate her feelings without saying something she shouldn't. "But not yet. I'm not free to do so."

"I see."

"No, you don't," she said quickly, noting his suddenly grim expression. "But one day I hope you will. Soon I hope I can tell you everything. I want to tell you everything. But right now I'm between a rock and a hard place—"

"Julie? Are you out here?"

At the sound of Dale's low voice coming from the other side of the tall boxwoods, hurt and betrayal flickered in Jonathan's eyes before the shutter slammed into place and closed off his emotions. Julie's heart took a nosedive. She groped for something to say. Yet before she could open her mouth, Dale emerged onto the path on her right and spotted her.

"There you are," he said, relief evident in his tone. "I've been looking for you everywhere. We have to talk—oh, hello, Mr. Taylor," he added uneasily, upon turning the corner and seeing Jonathan, who had been hidden by the tall hedge.

Jonathan didn't return the greeting. An icy frost covered his eyes as he narrowly studied Dale then Julie. "I think I get the picture," he said stiffly. "Yes, I see everything quite clearly now." A nerve jumped in his cheek, and he spun on his heel, away from her.

Julie opened her mouth to speak, to try to stop him, but what was there to say? Sadly she watched Jonathan head toward the house. If he had harbored any feelings for her, they had been extinguished now.

"Sorry, Boss. Guess that was really bad timing on my part, huh?"

Dale's soft query brought tears to Julie's eyes, but she blinked them back. His hand went to her shoulder in a comforting gesture. "Forget about him, Jules. After what I have to tell you, you may thank me for the interruption."

She turned and looked at him sharply. "What do you mean?"

"Aren't the kids with their tutor?"

Julie nodded. "I promised to play a game with them later, though. After they finish their studies."

"Okay. But right now you have a strong craving for fast food. Ask to borrow the car. In about half an hour I'll take a taxi and meet you in town at McDonald's."

"What's up, Dale?" Julie asked, alert to the undertone of excitement in his voice.

"You'll know soon enough. But I'll tell you this right now. You're not going to like it."

With those enigmatic words he left her standing alone in the path.

⋆

Julie dipped a French fry into the pool of ketchup. The only evidence of her shattered calm could be spotted in her trembling fingers. "Negatives, huh?"

Dale nodded. "On the top shelf of his closet in a sealed envelope marked 'Taylor.' Obviously Clancy wasn't too concerned about getting caught," he said around a mouthful of burger. "It was in plain sight—not even closed away in a box."

Julie sighed. "So Clancy has some negatives—big deal. That's hardly proof implicating Jonathan or giving him a motive to kill his wife."

"Ah, but not just any negatives, Jules. Negatives of Jonathan's wife in, shall we say, compromising positions, if you get my drift." At Julie's puzzled look he continued, "I didn't want anyone to get wind of what I had, so I went to the photo lab at the local university and developed the pictures myself—"

"You mean you just walked on campus without anyone asking what you were doing there?" Julie interrupted, her eyes wide.

"Hey, I look young enough to pass for a student, and I've found from past experience if I act like I belong at a given place, then no questions are asked. If anyone were to ask what I was doing, I would have said I was working on an assignment. No big deal." He gave a careless shrug.

Julie groaned. "You're going to force me to bail you out of jail yet, aren't you, Dale?"

A mischievous grin turned up the corners of his mouth. "Well, let's just say I was really glad a professor didn't happen by. Had he seen what came out of the developing tank,

I would've been expelled."

To Julie's chagrin, he took a bite of his burger and chewed it slowly. Glaring at him, she drummed her nails on the table.

"Aren't you going to eat?" he asked, his mouth full.

"Dale, if you don't tell me what was in those negatives—pronto—you will be wearing that vanilla shake."

He nodded, a glint of amusement in his eyes. "Glossy black and white photos of Angela Taylor with a strange man—definitely not her husband, though the image is blurred in spots and the face is never shown. It's someone with fair hair, though."

"Where are they?" Julie demanded softly. "I want to see them."

He wiped his mouth with a paper napkin. "No, Boss. Trust me on this one. You don't."

"Dale—"

His eyes grew serious, the fun-loving look in them gone. "Those pictures would have fit in with any hard porn magazine on the market." At Julie's soft gasp he nodded. "I suspect Clancy was anonymously blackmailing Jonathan Taylor about his wife. My guess is that Clancy took pictures of the missus without her knowledge, threatening to contact the media if Jonathan didn't pay up."

"But why Jonathan?"

"Jonathan Taylor was news, even before his wife's murder. And he has money—a lot of it. He's fair game. Something an ex-convict with a record for blackmail couldn't pass up. Also, if you remember from the bio, Jonathan's uncle was running for the Senate at the time. A family scandal might have hurt his campaign, though in today's society I doubt it."

Julie sighed and stabbed another French fry into the ketchup. She bit off the end angrily. "It still doesn't make sense. When I talked with Clancy, he seemed like the last person who'd want to do Angela harm by exposing her."

Suddenly she straightened up on the hard orange bench. "Here's a thought—suppose Clancy and Angela had an affair, and Clancy fell hard for her and then threatened to go to her husband with the pictures if she didn't leave him for Clancy. Suppose she refused, and Clancy did send the pictures to Jonathan. Angela confronted Clancy, and the two fought—and later that night she and Jonathan fought about the same thing. Then suppose Clancy was jealous—realizing he wasn't going to get Angela or her money. He waited for an opportune moment—then bam! He got rid of her."

Julie hit the table with the palm of her hand for emphasis, drawing curious stares from several diners. Feeling her face warm, she quickly picked up her Coke and took a drink through the straw.

"That's a lot of supposing, Boss," Dale said finally. "But it's worth looking into."

"And here's another scenario for you. What if Angela knew about Clancy's prison record, but Jonathan didn't? What if she threatened to ruin Clancy if he said anything to Jonathan about the pictures? And Clancy didn't want to take the chance of that happening? So he killed her."

Julie settled back. "As for trying to bump me off, anyone could have gained access to the staff's stairway—the outside door on the first floor is never locked from what I've seen. So virtually anyone could have pushed that urn off the balcony and escaped back down the stairway—Clancy, Sean— even Bessie Lou could have trespassed onto the grounds and accessed those stairs. Though I doubt she's our murderer."

"It's possible," Dale amended with a slow nod. His sober eyes lifted to hers. "But you realize, Jules, in light of this new evidence—we now have a strong motive for Jonathan murdering his wife."

Julie looked down at her burger. During her quiet times with God this past week, she had felt Him pressing her to dig deeper, telling her—not so much in an audible voice, but as a peaceful assurance deep within her spirit—that all truth had not yet been uncovered.

"He didn't do it, Dale," she said softly before gathering up her uneaten food. Ignoring the skeptical look in his eyes, she left the table, threw the trash in a nearby receptacle and walked out the glass door without a backward glance.

ᴥ

"Hey! You can't do that," Jon whined as Emily set his little blue man in the beginning spot with a triumphant smile. "You've sent me back eight times already!"

"There's no rule saying I can't," Emily said, moving her red captor ahead the bonus twenty spaces. "Is there, Miss Julie?"

"Hmm?" Julie brought her attention back to the Parcheesi game in progress. Forcing her mind to the present she replied, "No, there's no rule stating such a thing, Emily. But there is such a thing as mercy." She gave Emily a smile, taking any sting out of her words.

Jon reached for his container with the dice inside, but Emily stopped him. "I rolled doubles. Remember?"

Jon pulled a face, and Emily shook her cardboard cup dramatically and rolled a four and a six onto the board. Jon groaned. Julie could see that one of Emily's red men would land on Jon's space again if she separated the roll, putting all his men in the starting circle if Emily moved that piece. She already had two of her men at home—the finishing point of the game.

Green eyes momentarily lifted to Julie's, and Julie could tell the girl was having a hard time deciding what to do. Show mercy—or cream him? After a moment she let out a resigned breath then offered Julie a grudging smile before moving one of her men the full ten spaces. Jon gave a heartfelt sigh of relief, and Julie smothered a grin.

"Miss Rae?"

Julie looked up to see Mrs. Leighton standing in the door of the playroom. "Yes?"

"That man is on the phone again, asking for you."

"Oh. Please tell him I'm busy," Julie said, watching Jon take his turn. She picked up her cardboard cup, preparing to throw her dice.

"He's called three times today already," Mrs. Leighton said

in a disapproving tone. "And he's called every day for the past two weeks. Perhaps you should tell him yourself this time."

Julie met her cold gaze. She really didn't want to talk to Sean. She had spoken with him once, but all he tried to do was convince her to go out with him again. There had been no apology for his uncouth behavior. Julie decided it was better for her to keep her distance and let Dale take care of things on that end. "Thank you, Mrs. Leighton. Not today. Besides, Mr. Taylor is taking us out for a picnic soon."

The housekeeper compressed her lips and exited the room. Jon looked at Julie.

"I don't think she likes you," he said wisely. "She doesn't like Daddy either, so don't feel bad." He smiled. "But don't worry, Miss Julie—I like you."

"Me too." Emily gave her a shy smile. This was the first time Emily had spoken such a thing.

Julie felt tears rush to her eyes and held out her arms. "Come here, you two."

Both children scrambled to receive her hugs. Jon craned his neck upward. "Is Daddy really taking us for a drive later?"

Julie nodded. Since their altercation in the garden four days ago, Jonathan had been distant. His suggested outing had come as a surprise, and she hoped they might find a chance to talk, to be friends again. She dared not hope for anything more. Jonathan had walked away from the Lord, and though she was hopeful for his return and prayed for him daily, he was still under her investigation for murder. Two marks against any chance of a relationship between them. No matter that Julie didn't believe Jonathan guilty; she was undercover in his home, digging up facts. And when Jonathan discovered her true identity, Julie knew he would despise her.

To help alleviate her sudden despair, she gave the kids another hug then released them and cleared her throat. "If we're going to finish this game before your daddy comes, we'd better play."

❧

Julie took a deep breath of the pine-scented air. Something sharp grazed her upper arm, and her eyes opened wide in surprise.

Jon sheepishly looked her way. "Sorry, Miss Julie—I didn't mean to hit you. I meant to hit her." Turning his gaze on his sister, his mouth thinned, and he plucked up another white pine cone from the ground, making ready to throw his prickly weapon.

"Jon, you put that down right now," Jonathan said, his voice laced with authority. He slammed the trunk of the car shut. "I'll have no more of this!"

"She threw one at me! And make her stop calling me that!" Jon was so unlike his usual easygoing, cheerful self that Julie did a double take to make sure they'd brought the right boy.

"Calling you what?" Jonathan asked with irritation.

"A crybaby!"

"Well," Emily replied succinctly from behind the refuge of the thick trunk of a towering pine, "if the name fits, wear it. You did cry for five minutes straight after you lost the game."

"Did not!"

"Did so!"

"Did not!" Jon took a few threatening steps her way, moving his arm back to throw his weapon.

"I said that's enough!" Jonathan's powerful voice resonated in the cool air. "Jon, tell your sister you're sorry."

The boy turned on him, angry tears clouding his eyes. "You always take up for her! You never take up for me! I hate you!" Swiping at his wet cheeks, he turned and ran into the thick forest of trees.

"Jon, come back here!" Jonathan thundered.

The little boy continued to run until he was out of sight.

Emily turned to the two adults and blinked, her expression one of shock. "I'll find him. He's probably running home, since it's not far." Before anyone could say a word, she ran after him.

"Emily!"

The little girl didn't slow her pace.

Muttering, Jonathan opened the trunk and threw the picnic hamper back inside, then closed the hatch with a bang that shook the car. "She's right," he said to Julie. "The house isn't far. They'll be all right."

"All right?" Julie repeated incredulously. "Do you honestly believe they'll be all right?" She knew she shouldn't tread on forbidden ground, but the words broke loose, as if held in a pressure cooker and contained too long. "You didn't even give Jon the benefit of the doubt. You turned on him like it was all his fault. I heard Emily call him a crybaby. But you didn't want to hear what the boy had to say. You never do!"

Glaciers settled in the gray of his eyes. "I don't need you to tell me how to take care of my children."

"Take care of them? Ha! Now there's a laugh." Julie clenched her hands at her sides. "In the months I've been here, you've spent a whopping total of three days doing anything with them—and only a few hours at that! The children need a full-time father, not a walk-in who's only interested in spending time with them when it suits his purposes—"

"I said that's enough!"

"Not this time," she said, too mad to heed the fury boiling in his eyes, turning them to deep charcoal. "I've kept quiet long enough. It's time someone pointed things out to you, since you insist on remaining blind to your children's needs. Jon needs a father—someone who will take him fishing, listen to him, love him—do all the things with him that other fathers do with their little boys."

"Julie—"

"And Emily needs other little girls to play with. She needs friends as well as a father who gives her unconditional love. They both do. I've made some progress with her these past few days, but that girl has so much bitterness and confusion bottled up inside—I can see it in her drawings—and I'm afraid of what'll happen when it comes pouring out. I think that's what happened to Jon today. The dam finally burst. They both need counseling—especially after what happened to their mother. Those children shouldn't be forced to live their lives behind the walls of that big, gloomy house day in and day out—"

His jaw clenching with suppressed anger, Jonathan turned and headed for the driver's side of the car. Julie clutched his arm to stop him.

"Wait! I'm not finished—"

"Oh, yes, you are!" he said with emphasis and faced her, the forbidding look in his eyes giving deeper meaning to his words.

The blood boiling in her veins swiftly turned to ice. "What do you mean?" she rasped in a tight voice, though she already suspected she knew exactly what he meant.

"I want you out of my house tomorrow morning," he said sharply before turning away again. "I'll not have a nanny tell me how to raise my kids! You're fired."

She blinked and stood, watching as he wrenched the car door open, started the engine and drove away, wheels spinning in the dirt. She stared up at the cloudy sky above the towering white pines, dully noting it looked like rain. She should get back to the house soon if she didn't want to get caught in a downpour and risk the chance of getting sick again.

Dejected, she leaned against a tree trunk. "Now what am I going to do? I really blew it this time," she murmured, her hands going to her face. "Why couldn't I have kept my big mouth shut?"

She shook her head. Jonathan had needed to hear it. She was wrong to speak in anger, yes, but the words had needed to be said. If only she could have spoken them in love.

Sighing, Julie rose from the ground and headed through the trees in the direction of the house, hoping to outrace the coming storm.

twelve

A flash of lightning illuminated the window, capturing Julie's attention. She stopped packing and turned to stare at the square of black. Intermittent drops splashed against the dark pane, until suddenly, as if a mammoth bucket had been upended from the sky, the rain came down in torrents.

How could she leave this place and these people who had become so dear to her? Yet she had no alternative. And in leaving, she must empty herself of the strong love she felt for each of them. Already she knew that would be an impossible assignment.

Julie opened her door in case Emily or Jon cried out. Jon could usually sleep through anything, but when a thunderstorm awakened him, nothing would do unless Julie sang him a lullaby to help him get back to sleep. Who would sing to him after she was gone? To both of them? Who would play games with them and take them for picnics on the beach?

Julie sank to the mattress, moisture clouding her eyes. "Oh, Lord, it's just not fair. Why are the children always made to suffer for adults' mistakes?"

An image of their father came to mind. Julie dropped her hands to her lap, still clutching the folded blouse she'd been about to pack. There was a man who lived daily with his haunting memories. A man who had never been able to close them up in a box and live in the present.

A faraway, unearthly wail sounded outside the door. Icy prickles jumped on the back of Julie's neck before logic replaced fear. Emily.

Hurrying through the dark hallway to the girl's room, Julie found the girl in the throes of a nightmare. Julie put a hand to her shoulder and gently shook her. "Emily, Honey. Wake up!"

The child's eyes sprang open. She sobbed and reached for Julie. Julie smoothed her damp hair away.

"It was the dream. The night Mama died—" Emily blurted out then clamped her mouth shut. Turning her head away, she shook it.

"Tell me, Emily. What happened the night your mama died?"

"No. I just want it to go away!" she cried.

"It might help to talk about it, to share it with someone."

Emily said nothing, shaking her head more furiously. A nearby crash of thunder rocked the earth, and she flinched.

Julie picked up a stuffed orange-and-black striped cat from the floor and tucked it in Emily's arms. "You just hold Tigger real tight 'cause he's probably scared, too, and needs you to comfort him and give him a hug."

"Ju–lie!"

Julie sighed. "I need to go to Jon. I'll be back to check on you in a bit. Remember, Honey—Jesus is here with you. Just close your eyes and think of being held in His arms."

"Ju–lie!"

Julie tucked the sheet under Emily's chin and hurried to the next room. Jon sat up in bed, clutching his legs. "Sing to me?" he asked with pleading eyes.

Julie sat down and drew him near. She sang until his eyelids began to flicker shut then close. She laid him down and tiptoed away, but before she reached the door, he asked, "Can I have some calomile tea?"

"Jon," she said, turning from the door, "I thought you were asleep."

"Calomile tea helps me sleep better."

Julie grinned. "Oh, okay. One cup of Chamomile tea coming up."

Shaking her head, Julie closed his door partially and slipped into the dark hall. She felt her way along the wall, wishing she'd thought to turn on the light switch. It was on the other end of the stairway, several yards away. A door to one of the guest rooms had been left open, and bursts of blue-white light flickered into the darkness from the room's one window, because of the heightening storm.

A strange prickling sensation traveled along her nerve endings. Something was wrong, though she couldn't place what. She moved more carefully, her senses alert to any sign of trouble. As she reached the first step and turned to descend, she glimpsed a moving shadow from the corner of her eye.

Two hands pushed against her shoulder blades. Julie cried out, the thunder drowning the sound. She grabbed for the rail, managing to stop her plunge down the carpeted stairs. The unknown assailant came at her again. Julie turned to face her attacker, but even without the ski mask that disguised the person's features, it was too dark to tell who stood above her.

Julie grabbed the sturdy arm that was intent on pulling her hand from the rail and gave it a sharp, quick twist, sending the attacker to his knees. Bright incandescent light flooded the room. Julie dropped the assailant's arm in surprise. He took off running down the stairs—right into Dale's arms. The attacker struggled, trying to get away, but Dale tightened his hold, gripping him firmly across the stomach.

"Well, well," he said as he reached for the ski mask with his other hand. "Let's see who we have here."

A sharp crack of thunder rattled the walls. All electricity went out, plunging the room in darkness. Dale gave a surprised gasp of pain; then heavy footsteps clattered away on the parquet floor.

"Dale?" Julie cried softly as she groped her way down the stairs. "Are you okay?"

"I'll live." He groaned. "The jerk elbowed me in the eye and took off running."

Julie reached him and took his arm, leading him to the next room and a nearby window. Another flash of lightning through the thin draperies revealed his discolored left eye beginning to puff.

"Oh, Dale," she commiserated, her fingertips going to his cheekbone. He flinched. "You're going to have quite a shiner."

A white circle of light bounced off the walls and then trapped them in its steady glare. "I heard someone cry out," Jonathan said from behind the flashlight.

"Jonathan," she breathed. Realizing how it must look, she hastily lowered her hand from Dale's cheek. "There's been a bit of an accident," she offered lamely. "Dale got hurt."

Jonathan's face remained in shadows beyond the high-powered beam of the halogen flashlight. "An accident?" His tone showed he didn't believe her.

"Yeah, an accident," Dale replied dryly. "And Julie, here, almost met her death at the 'accident's' hands."

"Da–ale," Julie breathed in warning.

"What do you mean, Mr. Greenly? Explain yourself. And while you're at it, you can also explain what you're doing in my house at this time of night," Jonathan commanded in clipped tones.

Suddenly the electricity came back on, and the room was bathed in bright light. Jonathan flicked off the flashlight and turned his attention Dale's way. One eyebrow quirked upward.

"Exactly what *has* been going on here tonight?"

"I think before we proceed with further explanations, we should take care of Dale's eye," Julie said. "Then we can talk."

Jonathan shrugged. "You should find an ice pack in the freezer. It'll help the swelling, but the skin will probably be discolored for the next few days."

Julie thought she detected a satisfied note in Jonathan's voice and turned sharply toward him, but he had already turned away. "I'll meet you both in my office in five minutes," he said as he left the room. "I want some answers."

"He's not the only one," Dale muttered. He turned to Julie. "Let me handle this. I think it's better if you don't say anything."

Julie stared. "Why not?"

Dale rubbed a hand along the back of his neck, stalling. After a moment he looked at her, pity in his eyes. "He came from the direction the attacker disappeared to. It looks as if Jonathan Taylor is our man."

A loud clap of thunder emphasized his ominous words. Julie slowly shook her head and moved in the direction of the kitchen, trying to stifle the mantra that rang through her mind: He did it. . .he did it. . .he did it. . . .

"No," Julie said to the frozen goods before slamming the freezer door shut. "I refuse to believe it."

"Who are you talking to?" a huffy voice asked from behind. Julie spun around to come face-to-face with Shannon.

"No one. Just thinking aloud."

"You're not planning to eat now, are you? Cook's asleep, and I'm certainly not going to make anything." Shannon eyed the hard ice-gel pack in Julie's hands. "What's that for?"

"It's for Dale's eye."

"Dale's eye?" Shannon asked, her brow lifted. Annoyance replaced confusion. "Speaking of Dale, where is he? He was supposed to help me make a batch of cookies. I only left the room for ten minutes, and now he's gone."

"There was some excitement, and Dale got hurt trying to help me," Julie said guardedly.

Shannon's eyes simmered with dislike. "So Dale played superhero and saved your hide again, huh?"

"Something like that."

"Well, it looks to me as if someone's out to get you, Miss Rae. Maybe you should just leave this house before you get hurt." She walked to the door. "Tell Dale I'll talk to him later. With this storm it's probably not a good idea to try to make cookies now, anyway."

Julie watched her go, finding it interesting that Shannon knew about the attempt on Julie's life—though Julie hadn't said a word to her about it.

❧

"Okay, let me get this straight." Jonathan's eyes were sharp as he looked from Julie to Dale. "Someone tried to push Julie down the stairs, and you startled him by turning on the light. Then he tried to escape, and you nabbed him. When the electricity went out, he elbowed you in the eye and got away."

Dale nodded, holding the ice pack to his eye. "That's it exactly."

Jonathan fiddled with a ballpoint pen, tapping one end on the smooth wood of his desk with staccato beats. "Julie?" he addressed the slim instrument.

"Everything Dale said is true. When you came upon us, I was checking his eye. That's all I was doing," she said. Both men looked at her. Her face warmed, but she didn't turn away.

Jonathan straightened in his chair, dropped the pen, and reached for the phone. "Right. I suppose the next step is to notify the police." He put the receiver to his ear and frowned. "No dial tone. The storm must've knocked down the lines. And my cell phone is charging."

"I have one. In my room," Dale said, rising from his chair. "With your permission, Mr. Taylor?"

Steel gray eyes met unwavering hazel ones in a look of challenge. Jonathan gave a curt nod. "Go ahead."

After Dale left, an uncomfortable silence filled the room. Julie fidgeted, playing with the button on her blouse sleeve. Jonathan hadn't dismissed her, and she sensed he had more to say. He looked at her then.

"Julie—" He rubbed a hand through his hair, as though uneasy. Leaning forward, he clasped his hands on the desktop, his eyes solemn. "Before we go further, I want to apologize for earlier. I never should have left you alone in the woods with an impending storm in the forecast."

Julie shrugged, though she felt anything but nonchalant at the moment. "I got back before it blew in."

"I know. I watched for you."

"You did?" Her eyes widened at his soft admission. She had seen no one on her return and had only heard that the children were both safely in the playroom.

Jonathan leaned back in his swivel chair, the hinges creaking. He picked up the pen again, obviously uncomfortable. "I shouldn't have said what I did. I was angry at the time— but that's no excuse for my behavior. I know you hold the children's best interests at heart, and that's commendable. It was one of the reasons I hired you."

Julie's heart fluttered with hope. "Then—I'm not fired? I can stay?"

Instead of answering he turned away and stared at the dark curtains that glowed every now and then from the outside lightning. At last he spoke.

"Before tonight happened, I'd decided to talk to you at breakfast and ask you to stay. But now—now I think it best if you leave. You can go tomorrow after the storm clears."

"I would like to stay," Julie insisted.

"No." He swiveled in his chair, facing her. "I won't be responsible for anything happening to you. When I first saw that your life was threatened I should have dismissed you then. I was wrong to let it go this far."

"But—"

"You're to leave us tomorrow. And that's final."

"Nooo!"

Both Julie and Jonathan turned in surprise. Jon stood in his pajamas in the doorway, his raggedy teddy bear dangling from one hand. Shimmering tears formed in his eyes. "Don't make Julie go! Please, Daddy!"

Jonathan rose from his chair, his expression etched in stone. "What are you doing out of bed at this time of night? Go back to your room at once."

Ignoring his father's command Jon ran into the room and threw his arms around Julie's neck. "Please don't make her go," he cried, his hot tears wetting her blouse. "I love her, and—and she loves me."

"This matter doesn't concern you," Jonathan said impatiently. "It's between me and Miss Rae. Now get to bed."

"But, Daddy—"

"Now!"

Jon ran from the room, sobbing.

Julie turned on Jonathan. "Was that really necessary? The storm woke him, and he was waiting for me to bring him some tea and probably sing to him again," she said, rising from her chair and heading for the open doorway. "You know how he likes to be sung to sleep when storms wake him."

She turned to study him. "Come to think of it, maybe you don't. My guess is that you know very little about your son. Isn't that so, Jonathan? You treat him as if he were a stranger—and, believe me, he feels every bit of your indifference."

Seeing how Jonathan paled and how her sharp words pierced him, Julie turned and hurried away. Before she made it from the room, however, Shannon blocked her exit, almost running smack into Julie in her haste. The maid's anxious eyes sought out Jonathan, and fear lodged in Julie's throat.

"Mr. Taylor—it's Jon. He's run away!"

Jonathan stepped quickly around the desk to face the maid. "What do you mean, 'he's run away'?"

"I was on my way to my room when I saw him racing for the front door. I tried to stop him—but he'd already run outside by the time I got there. And I couldn't tell which way he went."

Scowling, Jonathan hurried from the room, the women following. He wrenched the closet door open.

"I'm sorry," Shannon said. "I didn't really think he'd go out there, as heavy as it's raining. And normally he wouldn't have, I'm sure—but he just seemed so upset."

Julie reached for her yellow raincoat hanging next to Jonathan's black slicker. He turned his head her way.

"What do you think you're doing?"

"I'm going with you."

"No, you're not. It's my fault he's out there, and I'm the one who should look for him. He can't have gotten far in this storm. You stay here in case Emily wakes up."

Julie faced him, ready to do battle. He did likewise as he shrugged into his slicker. Extreme worry and guilt clouded his eyes. The arguments died before they ever left her lips.

"Please, Julie. I don't want you out there in this."

She gave a reluctant nod, and he started to move away. She

put a hand to his arm, stopping him. He looked at her with a frown.

"God go with you, Jonathan. I'll be praying—for both of you," she added softly.

Something moist glimmered in his eyes. "You do that, Julie," he said, his voice gruff. "You do that." Turning, he hurried out into the raging storm.

"Dear sweet Jesus, help him," Julie murmured. "Help him to find Jon and see that You're not his adversary."

Feeling the need to check on Emily, she headed upstairs. She hoped all the excitement hadn't kept the girl awake. But surely, if she'd heard any of it, she would have gone downstairs to investigate.

The child lay sleeping, holding her stuffed cat close. Julie strode to the bed and carefully replaced the sheet that lay bunched around Emily's legs. She looked down at the sweet face, so peaceful in repose, knowing it was the last time she would do so. Tomorrow she would be gone.

Saddened by the thought, Julie turned out the overhead light, leaving the soft glow of the bedside lamp on. Before hurrying downstairs, she made a quick trip to her room for her Bible. She took up vigil in the library and glanced at the clock on the wall. Ten minutes had passed since Jonathan left.

What was taking so long? Couldn't he find Jon? Had one of them been hurt? She wished she hadn't promised to remain behind. And where was Dale? He should have returned by now.

Opening the Bible, she sought consolation from the words within. Her eyes caught and held a portion of Scripture in the fifth chapter of First Peter: "Humble yourselves, therefore, under God's mighty hand, that he may lift you up in due time. Cast all your anxiety on him because he cares for you."

She paused and thought about what the last part meant. God cared for her, as He cared for Jonathan, Jon, and Emily. Everyone she loved, He loved so much more. God didn't want her carrying the heavy load of worry when He was ready and willing to take her burdens. Relief washed through her as she gladly gave the weighty and unwanted loads she had been toting to her Deliverer.

Again she began to pray, but this time her words were ones of sure faith, rather than fear-filled pleadings of worry. She knew her Father in heaven would take care of the man she loved and the boy she had come to think of as her own.

Minutes later, when she heard footsteps behind her, Julie stood and turned expectantly, certain Jonathan had returned with Jon. Her eyes widened as she stared down the barrel of a .38 pointed straight at her heart.

"At last I have you where I want you, Miss Rae."

thirteen

Feeling suddenly numb, Julie reached for the chair back for support. The tinny taste of fear filled her mouth. She relived a similar moment when she had come face-to-face with one of America's most wanted, Stephen Cordova, and his automatic.

Mrs. Leighton, wearing a long raincoat and gloves, motioned her to sit back down and closed the door. Julie obeyed, her eyes on the gun. "Why—why would you want to kill me?"

The woman gave a harsh laugh. "You've become important to too many people. You should have heeded that first warning and left while you had the chance."

Julie thought hard, trying to think of a way to buy time. It was best to keep the woman talking. "And did you also kill your niece Angela?"

"Shut up!" Pain distorted the woman's features, and the hand holding the gun trembled. "I loved Angela. She meant the world to me."

"Yes, you did love her, didn't you?" Julie said thoughtfully, slowly, trying to piece it all together. "You even made a shrine to her to keep her memory alive. And you made sure Jonathan saw the painting he'd ordered you to destroy more than a year ago—to remind him of the past he was trying so hard to forget. So you left the door open, hoping he would go inside, never dreaming Emily would be the one to enter that room."

Patches of white showed around Mrs. Leighton's mouth. "You're smart, Miss Rae—I'll give you that. But your knowledge won't help you now. You never should have come here," she added. "Everything was fine until you showed up!"

"That's not true," Julie argued quietly. "Both children are still suffering from what happened that night. And Jonathan is suffering too."

"He deserves to suffer," the woman hissed. "He ruined Angela's life. If he'd paid more attention to her instead of always running off on business trips, she never would have turned to that no good drifter or others for love and affection."

"No good drifter," Julie repeated. "You mean Sean Mac-Phearson. He was involved with your niece, wasn't he?"

The woman snorted, her eyes narrowing. "He was unworthy of Angela! She had everything a woman could want—except for the love of her husband, that is—and Sean came along, turning her head with his charm, promising her things he never would have given. She even helped him buy a yacht, giving him a great deal of her money to do it!" She shook her head at the memory. "Angela told me she was going away with Sean to one of his islands and divorcing Jonathan, a few days before—before—" She broke off, a catch in her voice.

"Before she drowned," Julie finished. A new thought struck. "It was Sean's rowboat from the *Angel Dawn* that she took that night, wasn't it? A yacht would have been too big for that narrow inlet, so he must have taken a rowboat to the private cove for their trysts. My guess is that when he was in town, he anchored his yacht near the inlet."

The woman paled but didn't answer.

Julie thought frantically of all she had learned tonight and in past months and groped for something that sounded plausible—anything to keep the woman from shooting. "Sean was usually the one to use the rowboat, coming to see Angela. But they had secretly arranged for Angela to take the boat to his yacht that night, so she could go away with him. He must have left the rowboat for her at the cove when he went to town. After his friends dropped him off at his yacht, once the storm was over, and she hadn't shown, he probably thought she'd changed her mind. So he set sail early the next morning without her—"

"Stop it—I don't want to hear any more!" Mrs. Leighton declared. "It never should have happened like that—"

And suddenly Julie knew.

"You knocked the hole in the boat," she said slowly, "hoping when the danger was realized, it would be too late and the boat would be far from shore. Too far to reach safety. But you didn't know your niece would be the one to use the rowboat that night—and in a storm too."

Julie sat back in shock. "You never meant to kill Angela—you meant to kill Sean."

The woman seemed to wilt before Julie's eyes. "I was only trying to protect her from him. He never would have married her. He would have destroyed her, just as her father destroyed me."

"Destroyed you?"

The woman nodded, sinking to the opposite chair as if her legs could no longer support her. Her gun still trained on Julie, she took a deep breath.

"Angela was my daughter," she admitted, her face looking as if it had aged ten years. "I was only trying to protect my child."

Julie's eyes widened. "Your daughter?"

She nodded. "I told her the truth about her father. That he was a no-good jerk, a sailor—who used me—promising me love and marriage—then abandoned me and found another woman in another port." Bitterness laced her tone. "When I discovered I was pregnant, my married sister offered to adopt and raise my child. I agreed, not knowing what else to do. My parents were strict, and I was afraid of what they'd do if they found out I was pregnant. I was young and alone and had no job.

"I went to stay with my sister and her husband until the baby came. I've never trusted a man since, and let me tell you—Sean is the exact duplicate of what Angela's father was! All honeyed charm and sweet talk and empty promises." Her eyes flamed. "And Jonathan's no better. He was engaged to my niece, Claire, then dumped her for Angela. I tried to warn her about Jonathan then, but Angela wouldn't listen."

Her eyes took on a faraway look. "And she didn't listen that night, either. She was upset after I told her the truth about her father, and that I was her mother, not her aunt. She kicked me out of her room and locked herself inside with a bottle of vodka. I had to act. I only meant to scare Sean away. The day before that, I sent him an unsigned note, telling him to stay away from Angela or he'd be sorry. The hole in the boat was only meant as a warning. Clancy told me he saw Sean in town that day, and I knew that meant his boat would be at the cove. Don't you see? I had to remove him from Angela's life and protect my baby."

Her voice cracked on the last word, and it took a few seconds for her to compose herself. She straightened, her face bitter. An ominous click sounded in the room, discernible over the dying storm, as she cocked the deadly weapon.

"And now, Miss Rae, it's time for you to die. You've infiltrated yourself into my grandchildren's hearts and turned them away from me. Even though they didn't know our true relationship, they used to come to me when they were hurting or needed help. I used to be the one to soothe Emily when she had nightmares. But then you interfered.

"And Jonathan doesn't deserve another woman in his life, not after what he did to Angela. I can see he's in love with you, but he'll never have you. He'll never find happiness—I'll see to that." She stood, keeping the gun trained on Julie. "It's too bad you didn't fall down the stairs earlier and keep it simple. I do hate messes." She motioned with her gun. "Outside, Miss Rae. We've wasted enough time."

"Surely you don't want to go to jail for murder?" Julie asked quickly, trying to buy a few more minutes. "Or be separated from Jon and Emily? This could never pass off as an accident."

"Not an accident, Miss Rae. A suicide. I heard that Jonathan fired you earlier today. Everyone will think you were so grieved to lose the man you love and your place with the children, especially so soon after losing your father. So you found the key to the locked cupboard with Jonathan's gun and shot yourself." The woman gave a dry chuckle. "Or better yet, I'll fix it to look like Jonathan shot you. This time he'll go to jail for sure."

Dismay filled Julie. What was taking Dale so long? She had to think—fast! "Did you know Jon's missing? He ran away. Jonathan went out in the storm to search for him. They should return any moment. You don't want to take the chance of your grandson seeing this, do you?"

Uncertainty crossed the woman's features, then anger. "You're lying. Jonathan is locked up in his office. Judging from his actions all week it's highly improbable he'll be leaving it for another two hours. And Jon is asleep in bed."

"No—Jon ran away. He heard me and Jonathan fighting, and Jonathan went after him—"

"If what you say is true, then you're to blame for my grandson's disappearance! You and Jonathan both. Outside, Miss Rae. Now."

Julie stood, her heart pounding. She remembered the feeling of helplessness that time in Stephen Cordova's living room, when he had trained his cocked gun on her. And now she was reliving the episode. Same scenario—different cast. Would the police crash through the door with Dale, as they had then? No, the phone lines were down. So was this the end?

God, help me—I cast all my burdens on You and know You care for me!

With her eyes scanning the room for a means of escape, Julie preceded the housekeeper slowly to the door leading to the garden. Suddenly the overhead lights flickered off and on twice; then the room was plunged into darkness.

Julie dove for the carpet and rolled, coming to a stop when she bumped into the chair. The startled housekeeper emptied bullets wildly into the wall, in the direction Julie had stood. The lights came on. Mrs. Leighton panicked and ran for the door. Julie heard a dull thud, then a yelp of pain. Cautiously she stood to see what had happened.

Mrs. Leighton lay on the floor, dazed, the gun knocked from her hand. A hard plastic ice pack sat on the ground beside her. Julie turned her head to the entrance. Dale grinned, his one open eye victorious.

"Dale," she said in relief. "Thank God you're back. I was wondering when you'd show."

"I can't take all the credit for this one, Jules," he admitted as he hurried across the room to apprehend the woman before she gathered her wits about her and tried to escape. "Shannon helped. After you were almost pushed downstairs, Shannon spotted someone wearing a ski mask running down the hall. She followed and watched the attacker enter a room and Mrs. Leighton come out. Shannon was suspicious and hunted me down to tell me about it."

"Shannon?" Julie said in disbelief. Her gaze went to the light switch where Shannon stood, looking uncomfortable.

"Yeah," Dale said. "After she told me, we came looking for you. While she worked the lights, I pitched the ice pack."

"It was no big deal," Shannon said, embarrassed. "I always knew the woman must be nuts."

"Well, I appreciate your help," Julie said. "And so does my chief operative."

"Your what?" Shannon frowned in confusion.

"Chief operative," Julie repeated. "Dale works for me. I'm a private investigator, and we've been working on this case."

A groan issued from Mrs. Leighton. "I should have known," she muttered. "You knew too much."

Shannon's eyes grew round. "You mean you and Dale aren't together?"

"No," Julie said. "My interest lies elsewhere."

Sudden memory of Jonathan and Jon came back full force, forgotten in the midst of the excitement. Julie sobered. "Mr. Taylor hasn't returned, has he?"

Shannon shook her head, and Julie realized the futility of her question. Had he been in the house, he would have come running to investigate the gunshots.

Dale rose from tying up Mrs. Leighton with the belt of her raincoat. With a handkerchief he grabbed the gun and moved it to a small table near the entryway. "Well, Boss, congratulations on another case solved. Is anything wrong?" he added, noting her serious expression.

Julie told him what had taken place before her encounter with the housekeeper. He nodded, his expression grim. "Shannon mentioned it earlier. Want me to look for them?"

"With one eye swollen shut?"

At the reminder he picked up the ice pack and put it back on his damaged face, eyeing Mrs. Leighton with disdain. "I don't mind searching, Jules. The storm isn't as bad as it was, and I could pick my way around. Especially if Shannon holds the flashlight for me."

This remark was met with a dazzling smile from the blond.

"Okay. What should we do about her?" Julie asked, with a nod to Mrs. Leighton.

"I was able to get in touch with the police. They should be here soon. Incidentally, Clancy's split."

"Split?"

"Yeah, you know. High-tailed it out of here, scrammed, vamoosed. Took everything—Angela's Corvette too. I already reported it to the police. I think Clancy realized his blackmailing days were over. He must have discovered the missing envelope with the negatives."

Julie only stared, trying to assimilate this new information.

"You okay?" Dale asked. He walked toward her, his eyes searching hers.

She nodded. "Deep down I know God is taking care of this mess."

He looked at her strangely, then grinned. "You know, Boss— you may be right about that. At least you were right about Jonathan. I'll never dispute that gut feeling of yours again."

Julie managed a grin. "Can I get that on tape?"

❧

After Dale and Shannon left to search for Jonathan and Jon, Julie walked over to the woman sitting on the floor, trussed up like a Thanksgiving turkey. Cloying bitterness threatened to swamp any compassion she felt toward her attacker, and Julie had to bite her tongue to keep from saying things she shouldn't. This woman had tried to kill her! And almost succeeded—three different times! She deserved whatever she got—and more.

There is such a thing as mercy.

Julie's recent words to Emily during the Parcheesi game came back to convict her. *But how, Lord? How can I show that woman mercy after all she's done? To me? To Jonathan? To the children?*

Memory of their previous conversation came to Julie. Mrs. Leighton had evidently never known love. And the one person to whom she'd given all her love was also the one person for whose death she'd been responsible—her very own child. What a heavy load to carry!

An image of Jesus on the cross, bloodied and beaten, came to Julie. He had forgiven those who put Him to death. Could she do less?

"Mrs. Leighton?" she finally said.

The woman turned hate-filled eyes her way.

"I'm sorry for all the pain you've suffered in your life." Julie took a deep breath. "And I forgive you for what you tried to do to me." Saying the words helped Julie feel better, and she even managed a small smile.

The woman's eyes widened before indifference swept across her face and she looked away.

The front door burst open, letting in wind and rain. Julie hurried to the foyer. A drenched Jonathan carried Jon, and two policemen followed. With alarm Julie noted the boy's unconscious form in the soaked pajamas, which had a few bloody stains and were torn. His feet were bare, and his face was pale.

"I found him near the pier," Jonathan said.

"Should we take him to the hospital?"

Jonathan shook his head, heading for the stairs. "I'll call for the doctor to come. We need to get him warm. He was out there a long time."

So were you, Julie thought, her heart wrenching at Jonathan's weary expression. Suddenly she noted that, under his dripping hair, his forehead was bleeding. She lifted a hand to his temple. "You're hurt!"

"I fell on the path. It'll keep until we take care of Jon."

If Julie had ever thought that Jonathan didn't love his son, she knew better now. His eyes radiated with concern and fear for the child in his arms.

"What did you do to my brother?"

At the angry and fearful cry they both turned. Her expression one of terror, Emily watched from the stairs. Jonathan moved toward her.

"Emily—"

"No!" she screeched, shrinking against the wall. "Don't touch me! Did you kill him? Just like you killed our mommy?"

Jonathan's face turned deathly pale, and for a minute Julie thought he would drop Jon. A policeman walked their way. "What's going on here?" he asked, his shrewd eyes looking them over. "Did I hear something about a murder?"

Julie took charge and stepped close to him. "May I speak with you privately, Officer?" He studied her, then nodded, and she took his arm and led him to the library while she explained. "There was an attempted murder. Mine. The perpetrator is in that room. There are two witnesses, and they'll tell you anything you need to know. I'll come to the station and make a statement as soon as everything here is under control."

"Didn't the girl say he killed her mother?"

"No, Jonathan Taylor didn't kill anyone. The person responsible for the death of his wife is in the library. So is the weapon that was used against me. I'll explain everything when I come to the station. I'm a private investigator," Julie added under her breath. "I've been working on this case."

"Oh, one of those," he said, leaving no doubt to Julie what he thought of her kind. He moved toward Mrs. Leighton, and Julie breathed a sigh of relief. Yet before she could leave the room, the woman's voice stopped her.

"Miss Rae?"

Julie turned.

"Please—" Mrs. Leighton struggled to say the word. "Let me know what the doctor says about Jon."

Julie again felt grudging sympathy for the housekeeper. "I will."

Mrs. Leighton gave a stiff nod and averted her gaze. The other officer came into the room. As he read the woman the Miranda rights, the first officer untied the belt from her hands and ankles then slapped handcuffs on her wrists.

Julie stood a moment to watch before moving upstairs.

Outside Jon's door, Emily stood wide-eyed, her face white. Now Julie understood what had been troubling the girl these many months.

Julie crouched beside the child and put a comforting hand to her shoulder. "Emily, your daddy didn't kill your mommy."

"But I heard them fight and say a lot of bad things to each other. And—and Mrs. Leighton told me he hated her and—" She broke off, tears clouding her eyes.

So the woman had poisoned her granddaughter's mind against her father, hoping to turn the child against him. Julie cupped Emily's chin in her hands, her gaze steady. "Mrs. Leighton lied, because she did a very bad thing and was afraid she would get caught. Your daddy sometimes gets mad—everybody does. But I promise you—he would never harm anyone. Do you understand?"

Uncertain green eyes studied Julie. "Then what happened to Jon?"

"He ran away because he thought I'd have to leave."

Emily was silent a moment. "Will you?"

"Not if I can help it," Julie said, her voice laced with determination. "Jon will be okay. You and I can pray for him. And then you need to get some sleep so you can help me take care of him tomorrow. He may have to stay in bed a few days."

"Okay." Emily looked away and back, as if she wanted to say something else but was afraid to. Julie studied her quizzically.

"Can I sleep with you tonight?" she finally asked.

Julie smiled. "I think that can be arranged. I may not be there for awhile, but you can go ahead and crawl into my bed. I'll tuck you in soon, and we'll say a prayer for Jon."

"Thank you, Miss Julie," the little girl breathed in relief and hugged her around the neck. "You're my friend."

Tears came to Julie's eyes as she watched Emily's retreating back, the whispered admission nestling deep within her heart. Rising, Julie opened the door to Jon's room. Color had returned to the boy's face, though his eyes were still closed.

Jonathan stood from kneeling beside the bed that was covered under a mountain of quilts. "I think he's going to be okay." He moved toward Julie and took her hand. "Thank you for everything."

"Me? You found him."

"But you opened my eyes to see what I couldn't. I don't know what I—we—would have done without you," he whispered, his expression full of gratitude.

Her throat constricted, Julie forced the words to come. "You may change your mind about me after what I have to tell you. When you find out the truth about who I am—"

Shannon came to the entrance. "Mr. Taylor? The doctor is here."

"We'll talk later," Jonathan said.

Frustrated, Julie nodded and followed him to the hallway. Jonathan was right. Confessions could come later. Right now, Jon came first.

fourteen

After assuring Jonathan that his boy was young and strong and would bounce back quickly, the doctor checked Jonathan's forehead. Jonathan refused care, however, saying it was only a minor flesh wound and not worth the bother. When he started to cough, the doctor admonished him to take a hot bath before he developed pneumonia. Jonathan complied, and Julie walked the doctor to the front door, receiving final instructions.

After Jonathan had dressed in jeans and a T-shirt, the most casual Julie had seen him, she insisted on tending his wound that had started to bleed lightly again and was surprised when he let her. His clothes made him seem vulnerable, shaving years off his appearance. Or maybe it was the uncertainty in his expression that reminded Julie of a hurt little boy whom she wanted to hold and soothe. She swabbed the cut on his forehead with antiseptic, pretending indifference to his steady gaze, though it shook her to the core.

"Chicken soup sounds like just the thing right now. Don't you think?" she asked.

Jonathan stared at her a moment longer then nodded, and they moved downstairs to the kitchen. Julie heated the soup in the microwave oven. Once the timer beeped, she poured the liquid into two large mugs and brought them to the table, setting one before Jonathan. He stared at the noodles and white flecks swimming in the tan liquid.

"Jonathan?" Concern laced her voice. "The doctor said Jon will be okay. Worst-case scenario would be that he develops a bad cold—though I wouldn't wish that on anyone," Julie added dryly, remembering her own episode with the cold bug months ago. "Still, it could be worse."

Jonathan nodded, his eyes distant. Julie touched the back of his hand, capturing his startled attention. "I owe you an apology for what I said in the library," she murmured. "It's obvious you're a man with a good heart who cares about his son."

To Julie's surprise he pushed his chair from the table and stood. Soup sloshed over both their mugs in the process. Rubbing a hand over his face, he moved a few steps away then turned to her, his eyes filled with self-loathing.

"I used to feed myself the same line, patting myself on the back for the great sacrifice I'd undertaken," he said bitterly. "But now I realize what a joke that was. My insufferable pride could have been the cause of an innocent child losing his life!"

Julie's brow creased in confusion. "I'm not sure I understand."

"So you haven't figured that one out yet, have you?" He shook his head, resigned. "I'm not Jon's father."

Julie stared.

"Angela sprang that bit of news on me the night we fought. Someone had sent me pictures of her with another man, blackmailing me, and I confronted her," he explained. "She poured herself another drink then as calmly as you please told me the truth about Jon and that she was running away with his father that evening and wanted a divorce."

If the chair hadn't been supporting Julie she would have fallen to the floor. Some detective she was! Thinking of Jon's twinkling blue eyes and mischievous grin, she realized now why Sean had seemed so familiar the first time she met him.

"Sean is Jon's father," she said quietly.

Jonathan nodded and sank back into his chair. Slumping over the table, he clasped his hands in front of him.

"Does he know about Jon?" she prodded.

"No." His reply was clipped. "Angela said she never told him. And considering the best interests of all involved, I felt it better to keep him ignorant of the fact."

Jonathan tipped his mug and looked into it. "I was extremely angry that night and called her some unpleasant names. She slapped me then ran out of the house and into the storm. I chased her awhile and then turned back to the house, disgusted. She was drunk, and I reasoned she'd come back soon. I was tired of playing her attention-getting games." He shook his head in remorse. "After they found her body washed up on the shore, I blamed myself for her death and felt guilty for the rotten husband I'd been. I felt I owed it to her to take care of her son and raise him as my own. Or so I told myself at the time," he said bitterly. "But the truth is that I was afraid people would somehow find out. And that would have brought scandal, as well as a huge blow to my over-inflated ego."

"That's why you quit going to church, isn't it?" Julie asked softly. "And why you never wanted the children to go. You were afraid the MacPhearsons might recognize Jon as their grandson."

Jonathan's gaze flew her way. "Partly," he admitted. "I also despised them because Sean was their son. By the way, he's the one responsible for the painting. Angela went to him years ago as a client to an artist then started seeing him on a more intimate basis. She told me everything—every facet of their on-again-off-again relationship—that last time we fought," he said harshly. "I'd only recently become a Christian, and being faced with the irrefutable proof of my wife's indiscretions and her subsequent death was more than I could take. Deep down I knew the MacPhearsons were nothing like their blackguard son, but I needed someone to vent my anger on. So I refused to have anything to do with them or their church."

"Oh, Jonathan," Julie whispered, tears filling her eyes at his pain. "What you don't realize is that by cutting yourself off from God, you cut yourself off from the only One who can heal your deep wounds. God cares about you—and, well, I believe He sent me here to help you. To help all of you— and maybe to help me find new meaning to life, also."

She sought for words. "You see, Jonathan—the fact is—" Julie released a soft breath. If she could stare down a gun barrel, she could do this. "I'm a, um—"

"Private investigator?" he inserted quietly.

Julie's heart froze. Her eyes felt as if they were being stretched in their sockets, as wide as they went. "You knew?"

He nodded. "I did a little investigating of my own after you arrived. I wasn't going to hire someone I knew nothing about to take care of the children. I confess I had the maid bring me your purse that first day, and I took the liberty of peeking at your driver's license. A few phone calls later, I discovered who you were."

"But—but why didn't you say something? Why didn't you tell me you knew?"

He shrugged. "No reason to."

"No reason to?" Julie repeated, dumbfounded.

"I thought it might complicate your investigation." He looked back into his mug. "I knew I wasn't guilty, and I've always wanted to know the truth about what happened to Angela. I never believed the ruling of accidental drowning—especially considering the hole in the boat. I thought Sean might have had something to do with it, and I wanted him nailed," he admitted, frowning.

Julie struggled to grasp all he was telling her, but she felt numb with the realization that he had known her identity all along.

"I'd heard reports that you were good at your job. You were good with the children. I knew you were honest that first day—when you didn't present me with phony references—something I'm sure Claire hadn't banked on when she played her little game of revenge against me by hiring you. Knowing her, she must have painted a terrible picture of me as a dangerous murderer and played on your sympathy concerning the children."

Julie swallowed, fiddling with her soup mug. "So you knew about that too." She lifted her gaze to his. "Are you angry with me for taking on Claire as my client?"

"Not at all. I thought I made that clear. I also wanted the truth about what happened that night."

He looked away again. "Earlier, when I was searching for Jon, I felt as if I'd entered some bizarre replay of that night with Angela—only this time it was her son I was searching for in the storm." He glanced at her, his expression remorseful. "Julie, I've been wrong. I blamed God for what happened, though deep down I knew it wasn't His fault. But bitterness was eating me up inside, keeping me away from the children, from friends and family—and especially from God. Out there—in the storm—" He broke off, moisture filling his eyes.

She reached out and covered his hand in a show of support.

Jonathan cleared his throat and continued. "Out there, guilt hammered at me for the way I've treated Jon. When I fell, the frightening thought that I'd never see him alive again shattered my pride, and I cried out, pleading with God to forgive me and save my son. It was then I realized I loved the boy, despite who his father is. I never could have lived with myself had something happened to Jon. And that realization brought another: God still saw me as His son, regardless of my failings and bitterness this past year. I again acknowledged Him as my Father and recommitted my life to Jesus."

Julie's heart leapt with joy. "Oh, Jonathan, that's wonderful!"

He nodded, his eyes bright. "I also promised God that if He would keep Jon safe, I would tell the MacPhearsons they have a grandson. And I intend to do just that, after church Sunday." He put his other hand over hers. "Will you go with me? It will be hard on them to learn what their son did—and I could use the support."

"I'll be there."

"Thank you." He smiled then shook his head in wonder. "You've always been there for me and the kids when we needed you—haven't you? It's too bad you couldn't discover what happened to Angela."

Julie blinked. "Oh, but—that's right. You were out looking for Jon, and when you returned it was all over."

"What was all over?"

She filled him in on the news concerning Mrs. Leighton and Clancy.

This time it was his turn to sit back, stunned. "Angela's mother? Well, that explains why the woman was so obsessed with Angela, though the feelings weren't mutual. Angela didn't want anyone to know Mrs. Leighton was her aunt." His mouth narrowed. "The news about Clancy being the blackmailer and stealing Angela's car doesn't surprise me. I probably should have fired him long ago, but he was good at his job, and I didn't want to break in a new chauffeur."

"The theft was reported to the police, so we should hear something soon."

Jonathan nodded. "I still can't believe Mrs. Leighton was the one behind those attempts on your life."

"I know. We never suspected her, because we were looking for Angela's murderer—not someone after Sean. Dale saved my hide tonight. Just as he came to my rescue on a case once in Florida."

A veiled look came into Jonathan's eyes as he pulled his hands from hers. "I didn't realize you knew Dale before I hired him."

"Dale works for me," Julie blurted out, realizing what he was thinking. "He's my operative and like the brother I never had."

"Your operative," he repeated.

"Yes—my operative."

"Like the brother you never had," he said and smiled slowly, sending warm prickles running through her. The smile faded. "What will you do now that the case is solved? Go back to Florida?"

"I hadn't planned that far. Actually, when Claire came to me, I was in the process of closing the agency."

Hope flickered in his eyes. "Then you don't intend to pursue your career as a private investigator?"

She shook her head. "It's not the same without my father. We were partners."

He took hold of her hand again and stood, bringing her up out of her chair along with him and causing her heart to race.

"By now you must know how I feel about you," he said softly. "You're like a light, warming me and opening me up to feel again." His expression grew serious. "Could you ever—I mean—would you consider—"

"Yes."

"Yes?" he said, taken aback by her quick reply.

"Yes, I'll marry you—that's what you were going to ask, wasn't it?" she added, suddenly apprehensive. What if she had misconstrued his nervous words?

His smile was both amused and relieved. "True. That's where I was going with it. But we Taylors are a very mixed-up family right now, and I don't think we should marry until things are straightened out—through counseling or whatever it takes." His brow lifted in question. "Are you sure you don't want to think on it and give me your answer later?"

"One of the rules of my trade. When you've got your man cornered—don't let him get away."

He chuckled and bent to kiss the tip of her nose. "I can see marriage to you is going to be an experience," he teased, before taking her in his arms for a real kiss that sent Julie's senses reeling.

"Daddy?" Jon's sleepy voice from behind startled them. They both turned to the boy, who clutched his teddy bear in one hand. "Does this mean you're not making Miss Julie go away?"

Jonathan rushed over to Jon and scooped the surprised youngster into his arms. "Never!" he declared, holding him close. "How are you feeling, Son?"

Jon blinked, obviously stunned to receive such affection from his father. "My knee still hurts where I fell down and scraped it." He lowered his head. "I'm sorry I said those mean things in the woods and then ran away tonight."

"All is forgiven," Jonathan assured him. "Let's not bring up the past again."

"Daddy?" Emily's voice was uncertain as she inched into the room while fiddling with the belt of her robe. Jonathan knelt and held his hand out to her. She hesitated then ran to him.

"I'm sorry for everything!" she cried, tears rolling down her cheeks as she clutched him tightly around the neck. "Miss Julie talked to me, and I know now you didn't do anything to hurt Mommy."

Intense relief swept across his face. He shut his eyes and held both children against him. "Of course, I didn't, Punkin." He looked up at Julie and stood, one child on each hip. "I would never hurt anyone I loved," he added softly.

Julie's face grew rosy. Emily looked back and forth between the two adults who continued to stare at one another. "Does this mean we're going to be a family again? And do things together," she asked, trying to get her father's attention. "Me and you and Jon?"

"Yes. And I thought we might add a new member sometime in the future." He looked at his daughter then. "I asked Julie to marry me, and she's agreed."

Jon squealed. "Then you'll be my mommy—won't you, Miss Julie?"

She nodded, accepting Jon's excited hug as Jonathan set the boy down. Emily still hadn't said a word. Anxious, Julie studied her. The girl stared back, a frown on her face. Julie hoped their tentative friendship hadn't been destroyed. It had been too soon to tell her, and from glancing at Jonathan's uneasy expression, Julie saw he realized the same thing.

"Emily, I don't want to take the place of your mother," Julie assured. "I know you loved her very much. But I'd like to be your friend if you'll let me. And I'd like to care for you as your mother would if she were here. I'm not great in the kitchen, and I don't have a lot of experience with kids, as you know. But maybe you could help me. We could help one another be a family."

Emily considered her words, then gave a small smile. "Okay."

Relieved, Julie hugged her.

"Look," Jon pointed to the window. "The sun's waking up!"

Jonathan stepped behind Julie, wrapping his free arm around her waist. He pulled her against him as they looked out the rain-streaked glass. "A new day," he whispered against her ear. "A new beginning."

Julie smiled and studied the brightening clouds laced with rose and gold. All vestiges of darkness had disappeared in the light of the rising sun. And like the sun did when it chased away the night, God had infiltrated this house, once filled with heavy darkness, and covered it with His bright beacon of truth.

Julie knew restoration and forgiveness would need to take place in all their lives. But at least they had reached the beginning of that road. And God would be there to lead them along the course of the journey.

Yes, it was, indeed, a new day.

epilogue

Two years later

Julie's arm tightened around Jonathan's waist. "Are you okay?"

He nodded, his sober gaze still on the *Bonny Lass*, which was moving out to sea.

"For what it's worth, I'm proud of the way you handled the situation. I know it wasn't easy."

Jonathan looked in her direction and attempted a smile. "I couldn't have done it without you. Or without God giving me the strength I needed."

Julie stood on tiptoe and gave him a quick kiss before turning her attention to the children playing on the shore. Emily and her friend Beth chased the surf. Jon set his toy boat on a wave that lapped up to his ankles. All parties felt it best that Jon know nothing about the proceedings of the past weeks, though it shocked both Julie and Jonathan to learn that Emily had known Jon's true parentage, having heard all Angela revealed that fateful night.

Weeks after Mrs. Leighton was taken to prison and Clancy was caught and put in jail, Emily admitted to Jonathan and Julie that she had fallen asleep on the loveseat in the alcove the night Angela drowned, and her parents' fighting had awakened her. They had been so upset with one another that they hadn't seen her there. Jonathan was heartbroken to realize his daughter had been in the room with them and had heard every horrible word spoken. Emily's main concern had been that Jon wasn't really her brother. Both Jonathan and Julie quickly assured her that Jon was, and always would be, her brother.

"Why so melancholy?" Jonathan asked softly.

"I was just thinking—how sad it is for Jon that his father

wanted nothing to do with him." Her gaze lifted to his. "But how wonderful it is for us that Sean signed the papers giving up any rights to the boy."

"Funny. I was just thinking the same thing."

Julie cupped his cheek in her hands. "And I was also thinking what a wonderful man you are not to deny the Mac-Phearsons the right to see their grandson as often as they like. Not everyone would have been so considerate under the circumstances."

"They're a nice couple," Jonathan said, obviously embarrassed by her praise. "They shouldn't suffer for their son's mistakes. Besides, it's obvious they love Jon, and he loves them."

"But not as much as he loves you," she said quietly. "You're his hero."

Jonathan's gaze went to the boy, who squatted in the surf and splashed his boat. "Ever since Angela gave birth to Jon and named him after me, he was mine, Julie. I grew to love him more than I could have ever thought possible. The same with Emily. When Angela told me the truth about Jon, it devastated me. I felt as if he had been ripped away from me. I kept my distance from him because I was hurt and didn't know how to act around him. As time passed he grew to look more like his biological father, which drove the knife deeper. But the main reason I kept Jon, and I can admit it now, was that deep down I never ceased to think of him as my son."

Julie felt tears wash her eyes and lifted her hand to wipe the moisture underneath Jonathan's lashes. He grinned wryly. "I've become an old softie."

"Well, that character description is preferable to the brooding man I met when I came here close to three years ago."

He cocked a brow. "Brooding?"

"Definitely. As dark and mysterious and handsome as a hero in a Gothic mystery."

Jonathan laughed. "You and those books you read."

"But almost from the beginning I knew you were no

murderer," she added. "The problem was in convincing everyone else."

"Thank you for believing in me." He sobered and drew her against his side. "Had you never come to Breakers Cove, I hate to think where we'd be now. I'm so thankful God sent you to be a part of our lives. I love you, Mrs. Taylor."

"And I love you." Julie gave him another kiss. "Shall we join the children?"

"One more minute." The color of his eyes softened to a misty gray. He gave her a longer kiss, one that almost turned her bones to liquid. When he lifted his head, he smiled. "From this day on we live in the present, with no painful memories hampering us. You, me, Emily, and Jon."

Julie gave a mock frown. "Is that all? I thought we might add to the list."

His grin grew wide. "Anytime you're ready."

"Okay. How about eight months from now? A Christmas baby would be nice."

Jonathan stared, his blank expression changing to one of shock as he caught on. "Julie—?" he said hoarsely.

She nodded, smiling. "I was going to wait and tell you after dinner when we were alone. But I think now is the best time."

"Are you sure?"

She chuckled. "Of course I'm sure. I was a P.I.—remember? I know how to spot the clues. Besides, I visited the doctor yesterday to confirm it. I never base a final decision on mere assumptions."

Laughing, Jonathan hugged her hard then lifted her up into his arms.

"Daddy?" Emily said, running up to them, Jon close behind. "Why are you carrying Mommy?"

Jonathan shared a look with Julie, one she easily read. Smiling, she nodded her assent. "Because you and Jon are going to get a little brother or sister for Christmas," he said. "And I was just showing Mommy how happy I was to hear it."

Jon shared a long look with Emily, and Julie tensed. They'd

come to love and accept her as their mother this past year. Surely they would embrace the news?

At last Jon turned their way, a hopeful look in his eyes. "Can I have a pirate outfit instead?"

Emily giggled. Jonathan grinned and carefully set Julie on her feet. A splashing fight ensued between all four of them, and laughter shook the air. Joy soaking her heart, Julie thanked God for the miracle of His healing love.

A Letter To Our Readers

Dear Reader:

In order that we might better contribute to your reading enjoyment, we would appreciate your taking a few minutes to respond to the following questions. We welcome your comments and read each form and letter we receive. When completed, please return to the following:

Rebecca Germany, Fiction Editor
Heartsong Presents
PO Box 719
Uhrichsville, Ohio 44683

1. Did you enjoy reading *Beacon of Truth* by Pamela Griffin?
   ❑ Very much! I would like to see more books
   by this author!
   ❑ Moderately. I would have enjoyed it more if

   _____

   _____

   _____

2. Are you a member of **Heartsong Presents**? Yes ❑ No ❑
   If no, where did you purchase this book?_____

   _____

3. How would you rate, on a scale from 1 (poor) to 5 (superior), the cover design?_____

4. On a scale from 1 (poor) to 10 (superior), please rate the following elements.

   _____ Heroine   _____ Plot

   _____ Hero   _____ Inspirational theme

   _____ Setting   _____ Secondary characters

5. These characters were special because _____

_____

_____

6. How has this book inspired your life? _____

_____

_____

7. What settings would you like to see covered in future **Heartsong Presents** books? _____

_____

_____

8. What are some inspirational themes you would like to see treated in future books? _____

_____

_____

9. Would you be interested in reading other **Heartsong Presents** titles?   Yes ❑   No ❑

10. Please check your age range:
    ❑ Under 18   ❑ 18-24   ❑ 25-34
    ❑ 35-45   ❑ 46-55   ❑ Over 55

Name _____

Occupation _____

Address _____

City _____ State _____ Zip _____

Email _____